⟨⟩ **W9-BDR-573**

"ENOUGH! PREPARE THE CRIMINAL FOR EXECUTION!"

"Wait!" Lafayette cried as the noose dropped around his neck. "Can't we settle this like gentlemen?"

A sudden silence fell. The sergeant was looking at the captain, who was frowning blackly at O'Leary.

"You demand the treatment accorded a gentleman! On what grounds?"

"I'm Sir Lafayette O'Leary, a—a charter member of the National Geographic Society!"

"Looks like he's got something, Cap," the sergeant said. "With credentials like them, you can't hardly accord the guy short shrift."

"'Tis a parlous waste of time," the captain growled. "But—very well. Remove the rope."

"Well, I'm glad we're all going to be friends," Lafayette said. "Now, I—"

"Out pistols!"

"Wha—what are you going to do with those?" Lafayette inquired . . .

All things considered, he should have known better than to ask . . .

THE WORLD SHUFFLER

Ace Science Fiction Books by Keith Laumer

STAR COLONY

The Adventures of Lafayette O'Leary

THE TIME BENDER
THE WORLD SHUFFLER
THE SHAPE CHANGER
THE GALAXY BUILDER

THE WORLD SHUFFLER

KEITH LAUMER

ACE SCIENCE FICTION BOOKS
NEW YORK

THE WORLD SHUFFLER

An Ace Science Fiction Book / published by arrangement with
the author

PRINTING HISTORY
First Ace printing / April 1981
Fourth printing / April 1984

All rights reserved.
Copyright © 1970 by Keith Laumer
Cover art by Rowena
This book may not be reproduced in whole or in part,
by mimeograph or any other means, without permission.
For information address: The Berkley Publishing Group,
200 Madison Avenue, New York, N.Y. 10016.

ISBN: 0-441-91703-8

Ace Science Fiction Books are published by The Berkley Publishing Group,
200 Madison Avenue, New York, New York 10016.
PRINTED IN THE UNITED STATES OF AMERICA

One

It was a warm autumnal afternoon in Artesia. Lafayette O'Leary, late of the U.S.A., now Sir Lafayette O'Leary since his official investiture with knighthood by Princess Adoranne, was lounging at ease in a brocaded chair in his spacious library, beside a high, richly draped window overlooking the palace gardens. He was dressed in purple kneepants, a shirt of heavy white silk, gold-buckled shoes of glove-soft kid. A massive emerald winked on one finger beside the heavy silver ring bearing the device of the ax and dragon. A tall, cool drink stood at his elbow. From a battery of speakers concealed behind the hangings, a Debussy tone poem caressed the air.

O'Leary patted back a yawn and laid aside the book he had been idly leafing through. It was a thick, leatherbound volume on the Art of Bemusement, packed with fine print but, alas, deficient in specifics. For three years—ever since Central had relieved a bothersome probability stress among the continua by transferring him here from Colby Corners—he had been trying without visible success to regain his short-lived ability to focus the physical energies, as Professor Doctor Hans Joseph Schimmerkopf had put it in his massive tome on the Practice of Mesmerism. Now *that* had been a book you could get your teeth into, Lafayette reflected ruefully. And he'd only read part of chapter one. What a pity he hadn't had time to bring it along to Artesia. But things had been rather rushed, there at the last—and faced with a choice between Mrs. MacGlint's Clean Rooms and Board and a palace suite with Daphne, who would have hesitated?

Ah, those had been exciting days, Lafayette thought fondly. All those years, back in Colby Corners, he had suspected that life held more in store for him than the career of a penniless draftsman, subsisting on sardines and dreams. And then he had run across Professor Schimmerkopf's massive tome. The prose had been a bit old-fashioned, but the message was clear: with a little concentration, you could make your dreams come true—or at least *seem* true. And if by self-hypnosis you could turn your shabby bedroom into a damask-draped chamber full of perfumed night air and distant music—why not try it?

And try it he had—with astonishing success. He had imagined a quaint old street in a quaint old town—and presto! There he was, surrounded by all the sights and sounds and smells that rounded out the illusion. Even knowing it was all a self-induced dream hadn't lessened the marvel of it. And then, when things got rough, he had made another startling discovery: if it was a dream, he was stuck in it. Artesia was real—as real as Colby Corners. In fact, there were those who could argue that Colby Corners was the dream, from which he had awakened to find himself back in Artesia, where he really belonged.

Of course, it had taken a while to discover that this was his true spiritual home. For a while it had appeared that he'd discover the answer to the old question as to whether a man who dreamed he'd fallen off a cliff would ever wake up. In his case it hadn't been a cliff, of course—but that was about the only form of demise he hadn't been threatened with. First there had been Count Alain's challenge, and the duel from the consequences of which Daphne had saved him with a carefully placed chamber pot dropped at the psychological moment from an upper window of the palace; then King Goruble's insistence that he hunt down a dragon—in return for his neck. And after that, a whole series of threats to life and limb, ending with his dispatch of Lod, the two-headed giant. And then the discovery that Lod had been transported into Artesia from another plane, along with his pet allosaur—the dragon with which he had terrorized the countryside—all at the order of the false King Goruble.

It had been more luck than wisdom, Lafayette conceded privately, that had enabled him to prove that the usurper had murdered the former king and transported his infant heir to another continuum by use of the unauthorized Traveler he had brought along when defecting from his post as an agent of Central—the supreme authority in interdimensional matters. And he had been just in time to thwart Goruble's last-ditch attempt to secure his position by ridding himself of Princess Adoranne. It had been pure accident that Goruble, thinking himself mortally wounded, had confessed to Lafayette that he—O'Leary—was the true king of Artesia.

For a few moments there, the situation had been awkward indeed—and then Goruble had solved the problem of his own disposition by stumbling into the Traveler—which had instantly whisked him out of their lives, after which Lafayette had abdicated in favor of the princess, and settled down to a life of bliss with the sweet and faithful Daphne.

Lafayette sighed and rose, stood gazing out the window. Down in the palace gardens, some sort of afternoon tea party was under way. At least it *had* been under way; now that he thought of it, he hadn't heard the chattering and laughter for several minutes; and the paths and lawns were almost empty. A few last-departing guests strolled toward the gates; a lone butler was hurrying toward the kitchen with a tray of empty cups and plates and crumpled napkins. A maid in a short skirt that revealed a neat pair of legs was whisking cake crumbs from a marble table beside the fountain. The sight of her saucy costume gave Lafayette a pang of nostalgia. If he squinted his eyes a little, he could almost imagine it was Daphne as he had first known her. Somehow, he thought with a touch of melancholy, it had all been gayer then, brighter, simpler. Of course, there had been a few drawbacks: Old King Goruble had been pretty intent on cutting his head off, and Lod the Giant had had similar ideas; and there had been the business of disposing of the dragon, to say nothing of the complicated problems of Count Alain and the Red Bull.

But now Lod and the dragon were dead—the bad dragon, that is. Lafayette's own pet iguanodon was still happily stabled in an abandoned powder house nearby, eating his usual twelve bales of fresh hay daily. Alain was married to Adoranne, and quite affable, now that there was nothing to be jealous about. And the Red Bull had published his memoirs and settled down to tavern-keeping in a quaint little inn called the One-Eyed Man at the edge of the capital. As for Goruble, there was no telling where he had ended up, since he had been so abruptly transported out of the dimension by his own Traveler. Daphne was still as cute and charming as ever, of course—what he saw of her. Her promotion from upstairs maid to countess hadn't gone to her head, precisely—but somehow these days it seemed that most of her time was taken up with the gay social whirl. It wasn't as if he actually wished he were a hunted fugitive again, and Daphne a palace servant with an unselfish passion for him, but . . .

Well, it did seem that nothing much ever happened these days—nothing except the usual schedule of gaiety, such as the formal dinner this evening. Lafayette sighed again. How nice it would be to just dine tête-à-tête with Daphne in some cozy hamburger joint, with a jukebox blaring comfortingly in the background, shutting out the world. . . .

He shook off the daydream. There were no hamburger joints in Artesia, no neon, no jukeboxes. But there *were* cozy little taverns with sooty beams and copper-bound ale kegs and roast haunches of venison, where a fellow could dine with his girl by the smoky light of tallow candles. And there was no reason they couldn't eat at one. They didn't *have* to participate in another glittering affair.

Suddenly excited, Lafayette started for the door, then turned into the next room, opened the closet door on a dazzling array of finery, grabbed a plum-colored coat with silver buttons. Not that he needed a coat in this weather, but protocol required it. If he appeared in public in shirtsleeves, people would stare, Daphne would be upset, Adoranne would raise her perfectly arched eyebrow . . . .

That was what it had settled down to, Lafayette thought as he pulled on the coat and hurried down the hall: conventional routine. Dull conformity. Ye Gods, wasn't that what he had wanted to get away from when he had been a penniless draftsman back in the States? Not that he wasn't in the States now, geographically, at least, he reminded himself. Artesia was situated in the same spot on the map as Colby Corners. It was just that it was another dimension, where things were supposed to *happen!*

But what had been happening lately? The Royal Ball, the Royal Hunt, the Royal Regatta. An endless succession of brilliant events, attended by brilliant society, making brilliant conversation.

So . . . what was wrong? Wasn't that what he'd dreamed of, back in the boardinghouse, opening sardines for the evening repast?

It was, he confessed sadly. And yet . . . and yet he was bored.

Bored. In Artesia, land of his dreams. Bored.

"But . . . there's no sense in it!" he exclaimed

aloud, descending the wide spiral staircase to the gilt-and-mirrored Grand Hall. "I've got everything I ever wanted—and what I haven't got, I can order sent up by Room Service! Daphne's as sweet a little bride as ever a man could imagine, and I have a choice of three spirited chargers in the Royal Stable, to say nothing of Dinny, and a two-hundred-suit wardrobe, and a banquet every night, and . . . and . . ."

He walked, echoing, across the polished red-and-black granite floor, filled with a sudden sense of weariness at the thought of tomorrow, of yet another banquet, yet another ball, another day and night of nonaccomplishment.

"But what do I want to accomplish?" he demanded aloud, striding past his reflection in the tall mirrors lining the hall. "The whole point in sweating over a job is to earn the cash to let you do what you want to do. And I'm already doing what I want to do." He glanced sideways at his image, splendid in plum and purple and gilt. "Aren't I?

"We'll go away," he muttered as he hurried toward the garden. "Up into the mountains, or out into the desert, maybe. Or to the seashore. I'll bet Daphne's never gone skinny-dipping in the moonlight. At least not with me. And we'll take along some supplies, and cook our own meals, and fish and bird-watch, and take botanical notes, and . . ."

He paused on the wide terrace, scanning the green expanse below for a glimpse of Daphne's slender, curvaceous figure. The last of the partygoers had gone; the butler had disappeared, and the maid. A single aged gardener puttered in a far corner.

Lafayette slowed, mooched along the path, hardly aware of the scent of gardenia in blossom, of the lazy hum of bees, the soft sigh of the breeze through well-tended treetops. His enthusiasm had drained away. What good would going away do? He'd still be the same Lafayette O'Leary, and Daphne would the same girl she was here. Probably after the first flush of enthusiasm he'd begin to miss his comfortable chair and well-stocked refrigerator, and Daphne would begin to fret over her hair-do and wonder what was going on in her absence from the party scene. And then there would be the insect bites and the hot sun and the cold nights and the burned food and all the other inconveniences he'd gotten used to doing without. . . .

A tall figure appeared briefly at the end of the path: Count Alain, hurrying somewhere. Lafayette called after him, but when he reached the cross path, there was no one in sight. He turned back, feeling definitely depressed now, he admitted. For the first time in three years he had the same old feeling he used to have back in Colby Corners, when he'd go for his evening walk around the block and watch the yellow twilight fade to darkness, thinking of all the things he'd do, someday . . .

Lafayette straightened his back. He was acting like a nitwit. He had the best deal in the world—in any world—and all he had to do was enjoy it. Why rock the boat? Dinner was in an hour. He'd go, as he always went, listen to the conversation he always listened to. But he didn't feel like going back inside—not just yet; he wasn't quite up to making bright conversation. He'd sit on his favorite marble bench for a while and read a page or two of the current issue of *Popular Thaumaturgy*, and think himself into a proper mood for the gay banter at the dinner table. He'd make it a point to tell Daphne how stunning she looked in her latest Artesian mode, and after dinner they'd steal away to their apartment, and . . .

Now that he thought of it, it had been quite a while since he had whispered an abandoned suggestion in Daphne's cute little ear. He'd been so busy with his wine, and holding up his end of the conversation, and of course Daphne was quite content to sit with the other court wives, discussing their tatting or whatever it was the ladies discussed, while the gentlemen quaffed brandy and smoked cigars and exchanged racy anecdotes.

Lafayette paused, frowning at the azalea bush before him. He'd been so immersed in his thinking that he'd walked right past his favorite corner of the garden—the one with the bench placed just so beside the flowering arbutus, and the soft tinkle of the fountain, and the deep shade of the big elms, and the view of smooth lawn sloping down to the poplars beside the lake. . . .

He walked back, found himself at the corner where he had glimpsed Alain. Funny He'd passed it again. He looked both ways along the empty paths, then shook his head and set off determinedly. Ten paces brought him to the wide walk leading back to the terrace.

"I'm losing my grip," he muttered. "I *know* it's the first turn past the fountain . . ." He halted, staring uncertainly across the strangely narrowed lawn. Fountain? There was no fountain in sight;

just the graveled path, littered with dead leaves, and the trees, and the brick wall at the other end. But the brick wall should be farther back, past several turns and a duck pond. Lafayette hurried on, around a turn. . . . The path ran out, became a foot-worn strip of dirt across untended weeds. He turned—and encountered a solid wall of shrubbery. Sharp twigs raked at him, ripping at his lace cuffs as he fought his way through, to emerge in a small patch of dandelion-pocked grass. There were no flowerbeds in sight. No benches. No paths. The palace had a desolate, unoccupied look, looming against a suddenly dull sky. The shuttered windows were like blind eyes; dead leaves blew across the terrace.

O'Leary went quickly up the terrace steps, through the French doors into the mirrored hall. Dust lay thick on the marble floor. His feet echoed as he crossed quickly to the guardroom, threw open the door. Except for an odor of stale bedding and mildew, it was empty.

Back in the corridor, Lafayette shouted. There was no answer. He tried doors, looked into empty rooms. He paused, cocked his head, listened, heard only the far-away twitter of a bird call.

"This is ridiculous," he heard himself saying aloud, fighting down a sinking feeling in the stomach. "Everyone can't have just picked up and sneaked out without even telling me. Daphne would never do a thing like that. . . ."

He started up the stairs, found himself taking them three at a time. The carpeting had been removed from the upper corridor, the walls stripped of the paintings of courtiers of bygone years. He flung wide his apartment door, stared at the unfurnished room, the drapeless windows.

"Good Lord, I've been robbed!" he gasped. He turned to the closet, almost banged his nose against the wall. There was no closet—and the wall was twelve feet closer than it should have been.

"Daphne!" he yelled, and dashed into the hall. It was definitely shorter than it had been, and the ceiling was lower. And it was dark; half the windows were missing. His shout echoed emptily. No one answered.

"Nicodaeus!" he gulped. "I'll have to telephone Nicodaeus at Central! He'll know what to do . . ." He darted along to the tower door, raced up the narrow, winding stone steps leading to the former Court Magician's laboratory. Nicodaeus was long gone, of course, recalled by Central for duty elsewhere; but there was still the telephone, locked in the cabinet on the wall; if only he could get there before . . . before . . . O'Leary thrust the thought aside. He didn't even want to think of the possibility that the cabinet might be empty.

Puffing hard, he reached the final landing and pushed through into the narrow, granite-walled chamber. There were the work benches, the shelves piled high with stuffed owls, alarm clocks, bottles, bits of wire, odd-shaped assemblies of copper and brass and crystal. Under the high, cobwebbed ceiling, the gilded skeleton, now mantled with dust, dangled on its wire before the long, black, crackle-finished panel set with dials and gauges, now dark and silent. Lafayette turned to the locked cabinet beside the door, fumbled out a small golden key, fitted it into the keyhole; he held his breath, and opened the door. With a hiss of relief, he grabbed up the old-fashioned brass-mounted telephone inside. Faint and far away came a wavering dial tone.

O'Leary moistened dry lips, frowning in concentration: "Nine, five, three, four, nine, oh, oh, two, one, one," he dialed, mouthing the numbers.

There were cracklings on the wire. Lafayette felt the floor stir under him. He looked down; the rough stone slabs had been replaced by equally rough-hewn wood planks.

"Ring, blast it," he groaned. He jiggled the hook, was rewarded by soft electrical poppings.

"Somebody answer!" he yelped. "You're my last hope!"

A draft of cool air riffled his hair. He whirled, saw that he now stood in a roofless chamber, empty of everything but scattered leaves and bird droppings. Even as he watched, the quality of the light changed; he whirled back; the wall against which the cabinet had been mounted was gone, replaced by a single post. There was a tug at his hand, and he continued the spin, made a frantic grab for the telephone, now resting precariously on one arm of a rickety windmill, at the top of which he seemed to be perched. Grabbing for support as the structure swayed in the chill wind, creaking, he looked down at what appeared to be a carelessly tended cabbage patch.

"Central!" he yelled through a throat suddenly as tight as though a hand had closed about it. "You can't leave me here like this!" He rattled the instrument frantically. Nothing happened.

After three more tries he hung the phone up

with dazed care, as if it were made of eggshells. Clinging to his high perch, he stared out across the landscape of bramble-covered hillside toward a dilapidated town a quarter of a mile distant, no more than a sprawl of ramshackle buildings around the lake. The topography, he noted, was the same as that of Artesia—or of Colby Corners, for that matter—but gone were the towers and avenues and parks.

"Vanished!" he whispered. "Everything I was complaining about . . ." He stopped to swallow. "And everything I wasn't complaining about along with it. Daphne—our apartment—the palace—and it was almost dinnertime . . ."

The thought was accompanied by a sharp pang just below the middle button of the handsomely cut coat he had donned less than half an hour ago. He shivered. It was cold now, with night falling fast. He couldn't just perch here beside the dead phone. The first trick would be to get down to the ground, and then . . .

That was as far as his numbed mind cared to go for the moment. *First I'll think about the immediate problem,* he told himself. *Then, later, I'll think about what to do next.*

He tried putting a foot on the open-work vane beside him; it seemed remarkably limber, his knees remarkably wobbly. The rough wood rasped his hands. As he started out, the framework sank slowly under him, with much creaking. He had already worked up a light sweat, in spite of the chill wind. No doubt about it, the easy living had taken its toll, condition-wise. Gone were the days when he could rise at dawn, breakfast on sardines, do a full day's work over a hot drawing board, dine on sardines, and still have the energy for an evening of plastics experiments and penicillium cultures. As soon as he got out of this—if he ever got out of this—he'd have to give serious thought to reviving his interest in body-building, long walks, pre-dawn calisthenics, karate, judo, and a high-protein dieting. . . .

The ring was a light tinkle, almost lost against the open sky. Lafayette froze, hearing the echo in his mind, wondering if he had imagined it, or if it had been merely the tolling of a bell down in the village; or possibly the distant ding-dong of a cowbell, if there were any cows in the vicinity and they wore bells that went ding-dong. . . .

At the second ring, Lafayette broke two fingernails in his upward lunge; once his foot slipped, leaving him dangling momentarily by a one-handed grip, but he hardly noticed. A short instant later he had grabbed up the receiver, jammed it into his ear upside down.

"Hello?" he gasped. "Hello? Yes? Lafayette O'Leary speaking . . ." He quickly reversed the phone as a shrill squeaking came from the end near his mouth.

". . . This is Pratwick, Sub-Inspector of Continua," the chirping voice was saying. "Sorry to break in on your leisure time in this fashion, but an emergency has arisen here at Central and we're recalling certain key personnel to active duty for the duration. Now, according to our records, you're on standby status at Locus Alpha Nine-three, Plane V-87, Fox 22 1-b, otherwise known as Artesia. Is that correct?"

"Yes," Lafayette blurted. "That is, no—not exactly. You see—"

"Now, this situation requires that you abandon your interim identity at once and commence to operate underground, posing as an inmate of a maximum-security penal camp, doing ninety-nine years for aggravated mopery. Got it?"

"Look, Mr. Pratwick, you don't quite grasp the situation," O'Leary broke in hastily. "At the moment, I'm perched in a windmill—which seems to be all that's left of the royal palace—"

"Now, you'll report at once to the Undercover station located at the intersection of the palace sanitary main and the central municipal outflow, twelve feet under the Royal sewage-processing plant, two miles north of town. Is that clear? You'll be in disguise, of course: rags, fleas, that sort of thing. Our man there will smuggle you into the labor camp, after fitting you out with the necessary artificial calluses, manacles, and simulated scurvy sores—"

"Hold on!" Lafayette cried. "I can't undertake an undercover assignment in Artesia!"

"Why not?" The voice sounded surprised.

"Because I'm not in Artesia, confound it! I've been trying to tell you! I'm hanging on for dear life, a hundred feet above a wasteland! I mean, I was just strolling in the garden, and all of a sudden the bench disappeared, and then the rest of the garden, and—"

"You say you're not in Artesia?"

"Why don't you listen! Something terrible has happened—"

"Kindly answer yes or no," the sharp voice snapped. "Maybe you don't know there's an emergency on that could affect the entire continuum, including Artesia!"

"That's just the point!" O'Leary howled. "No! I'm NOT in Artesia—"

"Oops," the voice said briskly. "In that case, excuse the call—"

"Pratwick! Don't hang up!" O'Leary yelled. "You're my sole link with everything! I've got to have help! They're all gone, understand? Daphne, Adoranne, everybody! The palace, the town, the whole kingdom, for all I know—"

"Look here, fellow, suppose I put you on to Lost and Found, and—"

"You look! I helped you out once! Now it's your turn! Get me out of this fix and back to Artesia!"

"Out of the question," the crackly voice rapped. "We're only handling priority-nine items tonight, and you rate a weak three. Now—"

"You can't just abandon me here! Where's Nicodaeus? He'll tell you—"

"Nicodaeus was transferred to Locus Beta Two-oh, with the cover identity of a Capuchin monk engaged in alchemical research. He'll be out of circulation for the next twenty-eight years, give or take six months."

Lafayette groaned. "Can't you do anything?"

"Well—look here, O'Leary: I've just leafed through your record. It seems you're on the books for unauthorized use of Psychical Energies, up until we focused a Suppressor on you. Still, I see you did render valuable services, once upon a time. Now, I have no authority to lift the Suppressor, but just between the two of us—off the record, mind you—I can drop you a hint which may help you to help yourself. But don't let on I told you."

"Well—go ahead and drop it!"

"Ah—let's see: O.K., here goes: Mid knackwurst and pig's knuckles tho you may grope/There's only one kind that's tough as a rope/The favorite of millions from the Bronx to Miami/The key to the riddle is—Oh-oh, that's it, O'Leary. Chief Inspector's coming! Got to go! Good luck! Let us hear from you—if you survive, that is!"

"Wait a minute! You didn't say what the key to the riddle was!" Lafayette rattled the hook madly, but only the derisive buzz of the dial tone answered him. Then, with a sputter, the phone went dead. Lafayette groaned and hung up the receiver.

"Pig's knuckles," he muttered. "Knackwurst. That's all the thanks I get for all these years of loyal service, pretending to be totally absorbed in living with Daphne and wining and dining and riding to hounds, all the while holding myself in readiness for instant action, any time that infernal phone rang . . ."

He drew a deep breath and blinked.

"You're talking nonsense again, O'Leary," he told himself sternly. "Admit it: you've been having the time of your life for three years. You could have dialed Central anytime and volunteered for a hardship post, but you didn't. Now that things look rough, don't whine. Pull in your belt, assess the situation, and decide on a plan of action."

He looked down. The ground, now pooled in dusk, looked a long way below him.

"So—how do I start?" he asked himself. "What's the first step to take to remove oneself from a world and into another dimension?

"Of course, you boob!" he blurted with a sudden dawning hope. "The Psychical Energies! Isn't that how you got from Colby Corners to Artesia in the first place? And I'll have to cut out talking to myself," he added *sotto voce*. "People will think I've popped my cork."

Clinging to his perch, O'Leary closed his eyes, concentrated on recollecting Artesia, the smell and feel of the place, the romantic old streets clustered about the pennanted turrets of the palace, the taverns, the tall half-timbered houses and tiny, tidy shops, the cobbles and steam cars and forty-watt electric lights . . .

He opened one eye. No change. He was still in the top of a windmill; the barren slope below still led down to the bleak village by the lake. Back in Artesia, that lake was a mirror-surfaced pool on which swans floated among flowering lilies. Even in Colby Corners, it had been a neat enough pond, with only a few candy wrappers floating in it to remind you of civilization. Here, it had an oily, weed-grown look. As he watched, a woman waddled from the rear of a shack and tossed a bucket of slops into the water. Lafayette winced and tried again. He pictured Daphne's pert profile, the lumpy visage of Yockabump the Jester, Count Alain's square-cut shirt-ad features, Princess Adoranne's flawless patrician face and elegantly gowned figure . . .

Nothing. The telltale bump in the smooth flow of time failed to occur. Of course, he hadn't been able to make use of the Psychic Energies since Central had discovered that he was the culprit who had been creating probability stresses among the continua, and focused a Suppressor on him;

but he had hoped that here he might have regained his former power. And—

What was it that bureaucrat on the phone had said? Something about a clue? And then that gibberish he'd spouted about a riddle just before he'd hung up. Nothing in that for him. He was on his own, and the sooner he faced it the better.

"So—now what?" he demanded of the chill night air.

"For a start, get down out of this nest," he counseled himself. "Before you stiffen up and freeze to the crossarm."

With a last, regretful look at the telephone, Lafayette began the long descent to the ground.

It was almost full dark when Lafayette dropped the last ten feet into a dry thicket. Sniffing vigorously, he detected a pleasing aroma of fried onions emanating from the direction of the town. He fingered the coins in his pocket; he could find a suitable tavern and have a bite to eat and possibly a small flagon of wine to restore the nerves, and then set about making inquiries—discreet ones, of course. Just what he'd ask, he didn't know—but he'd think of something. He set off downslope, limping a bit from a slight sprain of the left ankle, twisted in the descent. He was getting fragile in his mature years. It seemed a long time ago that he had rushed about like an acrobat, climbing over roofs, swarming up ropes, battling cutpurses, taming dragons—and wooing and winning the fair Daphne. At the thought of her piquant face, a pang of dismay struck through him. What would she think when he turned up missing? Poor girl, she'd be broken-hearted, frantic with worry. . . .

Or would she? The way he'd been neglecting her lately, she might not even notice his absence for a few days. Probably at this moment she was being chattered at by one of the handsome young courtiers who hung around the palace, supposedly getting instruction in knightly ways, but actually spending their time idling over wine bottles, gambling, and wenching. . . .

Lafayette's fists tightened. They'd swoop down on poor, unprotected little Daphne like vultures as soon as they realized he was out of the way. Poor, innocent girl; she wouldn't know how to fend off those wily snakes-in-the-grass; she'd probably listen to some smooth line of chatter and—

"None of that," Lafayette reproved himself sharply. "Daphne is as true-blue as they come, even if she is a little deficient in prudery. Why, she'd knock the ears off the first slicker who made an improper advance!" She swung a broom for enough years to have a solid punch, too, and she'd kept that trim little figure in shape by plenty of riding and tennis and swimming, once she was promoted to the ranks of the aristocracy. Lafayette remembered her, neat and curvaceous in a scant swimsuit, poised on the end of the diving board—

"None of that, either," he commanded. "Keep your mind on the immediate problem—just as soon as you figure out what the immediate problem is," he added.

The town's main street was a crooked, unpaved, potholed path barely wide enough for a cart to navigate, well dotted with garbage heaps featuring old fruit rinds and eggshells—no tin cans here yet, he noted. Dim lights shone from oiled-parchment windows. One or two furtive-looking locals eyed him from the shadows before slinking into alleymouths even narrower and darker than the main drag. Ahead, a crudely painted sign creaked in the chill wind before a sagging door set two steps below street level. The device was a misshapen man in gray robes and tonsure, holding out a pot. YE BEGGAR'S BOLE was lettered in crooked Gothic characters above the figure. Lafayette felt a pang of melancholy, comparing this mean dive with the cozy aspect of the Ax and Dragon back in Artesia, where he had once been wont to spend convivial evenings with a group of cronies. . . .

Leaving Daphne at home alone, the realization struck him anew. "At least I *hope* she was alone," he groaned. "What a fool I was—but as soon as I get back, I'll make it all up to her. . . ." He swallowed the lump in his throat, ducked his head, and pushed through the low door into the public house.

Greasy smoke fogged the air, stung his eyes. An odor of sour beer struck his nostrils, mingled with the effluvia of charcoal and burned potatoes, plus other, less pleasing additives. He made his way across the uneven dirt floor, ducking his head under the low beams from which strings of dried leeks depended, to a sagging counter behind which a slim female in gray homespun and a soiled headscarf stood with her back to him, rubbing at a soot-blackened pot with a rag and humming under her breath.

"Ah . . . do you suppose I could get a bite to

eat?" he said. "Nothing elaborate, just a brace of partridge, a few artichoke hearts, and a nice light wine—say a Pouilly-Fuissé, about a fifty-nine . . ."

"Well," the woman said without turning. "At least you got a sense o' humor."

"Well, in that case just make it an omelet," Lafayette amended hastily. "Cheese and tuna will do nicely, I think—plus some hot toast and butter and a hearty ale."

"O.K.," the woman said. "Rib me. I'm laughing, ha-ha."

"Could you manage a ham sandwich?" Lafayette said, a hint of desperation in his voice. "Bavarian ham on Swiss rye is a favorite of mine—"

"Sausage and small beer," the serving wench said flatly. "Take it or leave it."

"I'll take it," Lafayette said quickly. "Well done, and no rind, please."

The woman turned, tucked a strand of pale hair behind her ear. "Hey, Hulk," she shouted. "Saw off a grunt, skin it, and burn it, the gent says."

Lafayette was staring at her wide blue eyes, her short, finely modeled nose, the uncombed but undoubtedly pale-blond curls on her forehead.

"Princess Adoranne!" he yelped. "How did you get here?"

Two

The barmaid gave Lafayette a tired look. "The name's Swinehild, mister," she said. "And how I got here's a long story."

"Adoranne—don't you know me? I'm Lafayette!" His voice rose to a squeak. "I talked to you just this morning, at breakfast!"

A sliding panel behind her banged open. An angry, square-jawed, regular-featured, but unshaven face peered out.

"Breakfast, hah?" it growled. "That calls for some explanation, bub!"

"Alain!" Lafayette cried. "You, too?"

"Whattya mean, me *too!*"

"I mean, I thought I was the only one— Adoranne and I, that is—of course I didn't realize until just now that she—I mean that you—"

"Two-timing me again, hey!" A long, muscular arm that went with the unshaven face made a grab for the girl, missed as she jumped aside and grabbed up a frying pan.

"Lay a hand on me, you big ape, and I'll scramble that grease spot you use for a brain," she screeched.

"Now, now, easy, Adoranne," Lafayette

soothed. "This is no time for a lovers' spat—"

"Lovers! Ha! If you knew what I'd been through with that slob—" She broke off as the subject of the discourse slammed through the swinging door from the kitchen. She skipped aside from his lunge, brought up the iron skillet, and slammed it, with a meaty thud, against the side of his uncombed head. He took two rubbery steps and sagged against the counter, his face six inches from Lafayette's.

"What'll it be, sport?" he murmured, and slid down out of view with a prodigious clatter. The girl tossed the makeshift weapon aside and favored Lafayette with an irate look.

"What's the idea getting him all upset?" she demanded. She frowned, looking him up and down. "Anyway, I don't remember you, Sol. Who are you? I'll bet I never two-timed him with you at all!"

"Surely you'd remember?" Lafayette gulped. "I mean—what's happened? How did you and Alain get into this pig sty? Where's the palace? And Daphne—have you seen Daphne?"

"Daffy? There's a bum with a couple screws missing goes by that name, comes in here sometimes to cadge drinks. I ain't seen him in a couple weeks—"

"Not daffy, Daphne. She's a girl—my wife, to be exact. She's small—but not too small, you understand—nice figure, cute face, dark, curly hair—"

"I'll go fer that," a deep voice said blurrily from the floor. "Just wait till I figure out which way this deck is slanting—"

The girl put her foot in Hulk's face and pushed.

"Sleep it off, ya bum," she muttered. She gave Lafayette an arch look and patted her back hair. "This dame got anything I ain't?" she inquired coolly.

"Adoranne! I'm talking about Daphne—the countess—my wife!"

"Oh, yeah, the countess. Well, to tell you the truth, Clyde, we don't see a lot o' the countess these days. We're too busy counting our pearls, you know how it is. Now, if you got no objection, I got some garbage to drag out back."

"Let me help you," Lafayette volunteered quickly.

"Skip it. I can handle him."

"Is he all right?" Lafayette rose and leaned across the counter to look down at the fallen chef.

"Hulk? You couldn't bust his skull with a horseshoe, even if the horse was still wearing it." She grabbed his heels and started backward through the swinging door.

"Adoranne—wait—listen to me—" Lafayette called, scrambling around the counter.

"I told you—Swinehild's the name. What's this Adder Ann jazz all about?"

"You really don't remember?" Lafayette stared at the familiar, beautiful face, so unfamiliarly smeared with soot and grease.

"I'm leveling with you, bub. Now, if you're done clowning, how's about clearing out of here so's I can close the joint up?"

"Isn't it a little early?"

Swinehild cocked an eyebrow. "You got other ideas in mind?"

"I have to talk to you!" Lafayette said desperately.

"It'll cost you," Swinehild said flatly.

"H-how much?"

"By the hour, or all night?"

"Well, it won't take but a few minutes to explain matters," Lafayette said eagerly. "Now, to begin with—"

"Wait a minute." The girl dropped Hulk's heels. "I got to slip into my working clothes."

"You're fine just as you are," Lafayette said hastily. "Now, as I was saying—"

"Are you trying to tell me my business, stranger?"

"No—that is, I'm not a stranger! We've known each other for years! Don't you remember the first time we met, at the ball King Goruble decreed to celebrate my agreeing to take on a little chore of dragon-slaying? You were wearing a blue dress with little bitty pearls on it, and you had a tiger cub on a leash—"

"Aw—you poor sucker," Swinehild said in sudden comprehension. "Your marbles is scrambled, huh? Why didn't you say so? Hey," she added, "when you said you wanted to talk, you really meant talk, huh?"

"Of course, what else? Now, look here, Adoranne: I don't know what's happened—some kind of hypnotic suggestion, maybe—but I'm sure with a little effort you could remember. Try hard, now: Picture a big, pink quartz palace, lots of knights and ladies in fancy costumes, your apartments in the west wing, done in pink and gold, and with a view of the gardens, the gay round of parties and fetes—"

"Slow down, bub." Swinehild took a bottle from under the bar, selected two cloudy glasses from the mismatched collection heaped in the wooden sink, and poured out two stiff drinks. She lifted her glass and sighed.

"Here's to you, mister. You're nutty as a couple of dancing squirrels, but you got a nifty delusional system working there, I'll say that for you." She tossed the shot back with a practiced twist of the wrist. Lafayette sampled his, winced at the pain, then swallowed it whole. Swinehild watched sympathetically as he fought to draw breath.

"I guess life in these parlous times is enough to drive any kind of sensitive guy off his wire. Where you from, anyway? Not from around here. You dress too fancy for that."

"Well, the fact is," Lafayette started, and paused. "The fact is, I don't quite know how to explain it," he finished in a hopeless tone. Suddenly, he was acutely aware of the pain of scratches and the ache of unaccustomedly stretched muscles, conscious of his urgent need of a good dinner and a hot bath and a warm bed.

Swinehild patted his hand with a hard little palm. "Well, don't worry about it, sugar. Maybe tomorrow everything'll look brighter. But I doubt it," she added, suddenly brisk again. She refilled her glass, drained it, placed the cork in the bottle, and drove it home with a blow of her palm. "It ain't going to get no better as long as that old goat Rodolpho's sitting on the ducal chair."

Lafayette poured his glass full and gulped it without noticing until the fiery stuff seared his throat.

"Listen," he gasped, "Maybe the best thing would be for you to fill me in a bit on the

background. I mean, I'm obviously not in Artesia
any longer. And yet there are certain obvious
parallels, such as you and Alain, and the general
lie of the land. Maybe I'll be able to detect some
useful analog and take it from there."

Swinehild scratched absently at her ribs. "Well,
what's to say? Up to a couple years ago, this used
to be a pretty fair duchy. I mean, we didn't have
much, but we got by, you know what I mean?
Then everything just kind of went from bad to
worse: taxes, regulations, rules. The cricket blight
took out the tobacco and pot crops, then the
plague of mildew spoiled the vintage two years
running, then the yeast famine: that knocked out
the ale. We squeaked by on imported rum until
that ran out. Since then it's been small beer and
groundhog sausage."

"Say, that reminds me," Lafayette said. "That
ground hog sounds good."

"Brother, you must be hungry." Swinehild recovered the skillet from behind the door, shook
up the coals in the grate, tossed a dubious-looking
patty of grayish meat into the melting grease.

"Tell me more about this Duke Rodolpho you
mentioned," Lafayette suggested.

"I only seen the bum once, as I was leaving the
ducal-guard barracks about three at the A.M.; vis-
iting a sick friend, you understand. The old boy
was taking a little stroll in the garden, and being
as it was early yet, I skinned over the fence and
tried to strike up a conversation. Not that his type
appeals to me. But I thought it might be a valuable
connection, like." Swinehild gave Lafayette a
look which might have been coy coming from
anyone else. "But the old goat gave me the swift

heave-ho," she finished, cracking an undersized egg with a sharp rap on the edge of the skillet. "He said something about me being young enough to be his niece, and yelled for the johns. I ask you, what kind of administration can you expect from an old buzzard with no more sporting instinct than that?"

"Hmm," Lafayette said thoughtfully. "Tell me, ah, Swinehild, how would I go about getting an audience with this duke?"

"Don't try it," the girl advised. "He's got a nasty reputation for throwing pests to the lions."

"If anybody knows what's going on here, it ought to be him," Lafayette mused. "You see, the way I have it figured out, Artesia hasn't really disappeared: I have."

Swinehild looked at him over her shoulder, tsked, and shook her head.

"And you not hardly more'n middle-aged," she said.

"Middle-aged? I'm not quite thirty," Lafayette pointed out. "Although I admit that tonight I feel a hundred and nine. Still, having a plan of action helps," He sniffed the crisping patty as Swinehild lifted it onto a chipped plate, added the brownish egg, and slid it in front of him.

"You *did* say ground hog?" he inquired dubiously, eyeing the offering askance.

"Groundhog is what I said. More power to you, mister. I could never choke the stuff back, myself."

"Look here, why don't you call me Lafayette?" he suggested, sampling the fare. Aside from a slight resemblance to library paste, it seemed to be tasteless—possibly a blessing in disguise.

"That's too long. How about Lafe?"

"Lafe sounds like some kind of hillbilly with one overall strap and no shoes," O'Leary protested.

"Listen, Lafe," Swinehild said sternly, planting an elbow in front of him and favoring him with a no-nonsense look. "The quicker you get over some o' them fancy ideas and kind of blend into the landscape around here, the better. If Rodolpho's men spot you as a stranger, they'll have you strung up on a curtain stretcher before you can say *habeas corpus*, tickling your secrets out of you with a cat-o'-nine tails."

"Secrets? What secrets? My life is an open book. I'm an innocent victim of circumstances—"

"Sure: you're just a harmless nut. But just try convincing Roldolpho of that. He's as suspicious as an old maid sniffing after-shave in the shower stall."

"I'm sure you're exaggerating," Lafayette said firmly, scraping his plate. "The straightforward approach is always best. I'll just go to him man to man, explain that I seem to have been accidentally shifted out of my proper universe by some unspecified circumstance, and ask him if he knows of anyone carrying on unauthorized experiments in psychical-energy manipulation. In fact," he went on, warming to his subject, "he might even be in touch with Central himself. In all likelihood there's a sub-inspector of continua on duty here, keeping an eye on things, and as soon as I explain matters—"

"You're going to tell him *that?*" Swinehild inquired. "Look, Lafe, it's nothing to me—but I wouldn't if I was you, get me?"

"I'll start first thing in the morning," Lafayette murmured, licking the plate. "Where did you say this duke maintains his establishment?"

"I didn't. But I might as well tell you, you'd find out anyway. The ducal keep is at the capital, about twenty miles west of here as the buzzard flies."

"Hmmm. That puts it at just about the position of Lod's H.Q. back in Artesia. Out in the desert, eh?" he asked the girl.

"Nix, bub. The city's on a island, in the middle o' Lonesome Lake."

"Fascinating how the water level varies from one continuum to another," Lafayette commented. "Back in Colby Corners, that whole area is under the bay. In Artesia, it's dry as the Sahara. Here, it seems to be somewhere between. Well, be that as it may, I'd better get some rest. Frankly, I'm not as used to all this excitement as I once was. Can you direct me to an inn, Swinehild? Nothing elaborate: a modest room with bath, preferably eastern exposure. I like waking up to a cheery dawn, you know—"

"I'll throw some fresh hay into the goat pen," Swinehild said. "Don't worry," she added at Lafayette's startled look. "It's empty since we ate the goat."

"You mean—there's no hotel in town?"

"For a guy with a chipped knob, you catch on quick. Come on." Swinehild led the way through the side door and along a rocky path that led back beside the sagging structure to a weed-choked gate. Lafayette followed, hugging himself as the cold wind cut at him.

"Just climb over," she suggested. "You can curl up in the shed if you want, no extra charge."

Lafayette peered through the gloom at the rusted scrap of sheet-metal roof slanting over a snarl of knee-high weeds, precariously supported by four rotting poles. He sniffed, detecting a distinct olfactory reminder of the former occupant.

"Couldn't you find me something a trifle more cozy?" Lafayette asked desperately. "I'd be forever in your debt."

"Not on your nickelodiodion, Jack," Swinehild said briskly. "Cash in advance. Two coppers for the meal, two more for the accommodations, and five for the conversation."

Lafayette dug in his pocket, came up with a handful of silver and gold coins. He handed over a fat Artesian fifty-cent piece. "Will that cover it?"

Swinehild eyed the coin on her palm, bit down on it, then stared at Lafayette.

"That's real silver," she whispered. "For sobbin' into your beer, why didn't you say you was loaded, Lafe—I mean Lafayette? Come on, dearie! For you, nothing but the best!"

O'Leary followed his guide back inside. She paused to light a candle, led the way up steep steps into a tiny room with a low ceiling, a patchwork-quilted cot, and a round window glazed with bottle bottoms, with a potted geranium on the sill. He sniffed cautiously, caught only a faint odor of Octagon soap.

"Capital," he beamed at the hostess. "This will do nicely. Now, if you'd just point out the bath? . . ."

"Tub under the bed. I'll fetch some hot water."

Lafayette dragged out the copper hip bath, pulled off his coat, sat on the bed to tug at his shoes. Beyond the window, the rising moon gleamed on the distant hills, so similar to the hills of home, and at the same time so different. Back in Artesia, Daphne was probably going in to dinner on the arm of some fast-talking dandy now, wondering where he was, possibly even dabbing away a few tears of loneliness. . . .

He wrenched his thoughts away from the mental picture of her slim cuddliness and drew a calming lungful of air. No point in getting all emotional again. After all, he was doing all he could. Tomorrow things would seem brighter. Where there's a will there's a way. Absence makes the heart grow fonder . . .

"Of me?" he muttered. "Or of somebody closer to the scene? . . ."

The door opened and Swinehild appeared, a steaming bucket in each hand. She poured them in the bath, tested it with her elbow.

"Just right," she said. He closed the door behind her, pulled off his clothes—the rich cloth was sadly ripped and snagged, he saw—and settled himself in the grateful warmth. There was no washcloth visible, but a lump of brown soap was ready to hand. He sudsed up, used his cupped palms to sluice water over his head, washing soap into his eyes. He sloshed vigorously, muttering to himself, rose, groping for a towel.

"Damn," he said, "I forgot to ask—"

"Here." Swinehild's voice spoke beside him; a rough cloth was pressed into his hand. O'Leary grabbed it and whipped it around himself.

"What are you doing here?" he demanded, stepping out onto the cold floor. He used a corner of the towel to clear an eye. The girl was just shedding a coarse cotton shift. "Here," O'Leary blurted. "What are you doing?"

"If you're through with the bathwater," she said tartly, "I'm taking a bath."

O'Leary swiftly averted his eyes—not for aesthetic reasons: quite the opposite. The quick flash he had gotten of her slender body, one toe dipped tentatively in the soapy water, had been remarkably pleasant. For all her straggly hair and chipped nails, Swinehild had a figure like a princess—like Princess Adoranne, to be precise. He mopped his back and chest quickly, gave a quick dab at his legs, turned back the covers, and hopped into the bed, pulling the quilt up to his chin.

Swinehild was humming softly to herself, splashing in a carefree way.

"Hurry up," he said, facing the wall. "What if Alain—I mean Hulk—walks in?"

"He'll just have to wait his turn," Swinehild said. "Not that he ever washes below the chin, the slob."

"He is your husband, isn't he?"

"You could call him that. We never had no magic words said over us, or even a crummy civil ceremony at the county seat, but you know how it is. It might remind somebody to put us on the tax rolls, he says, the bum, but if you ask me—"

"Almost finished?" O'Leary squeaked, screwing his eyes shut against a rising temptation to open them.

"Uh-huh. All done but my—"

"Please—I need my sleep if I'm going to cover all that ground tomorrow!"

"Where's the towel?"

"On the foot of the bed."

Soft sounds of feminine breathing, of brisk fric-
tion between coarse cloth and firm feminine flesh,
the pad of bare feminine feet—

"Move over," a soft feminine voice breathed in
his ear.

"What?" Lafayette sat bolt upright. "Good lord,
Swinehild, you can't sleep here!"

"You're telling me I can't sleep in my own
bed?" she demanded indignantly. "You expect
me to bed down in the goat pen?"

"No—of course not—but . . ."

"Look, Lafe, it's share and share alike, or you
can go sleep on the kitchen table, silver piece or
no silver piece." He felt her warm, smooth body
slide in next to him, lean across him to blow out
the candle.

"That's not the point," Lafayette said weakly.
"The point is . . ."

"Yeah?"

"Well, I can't seem to remember the point right
now. All I know is that this is a very chancy
situation, with your hubby snoring downstairs
and only one way out of here."   ·

"Speaking of snoring," Swinehild said suddenly. "I haven't heard a sound for the last five
minutes—"

With a crash of splintering wood, the door burst
open. By the light of an oil lantern held high,
Lafayette saw the enraged visage of Hulk, ren-
dered no less fierce by a well-blacked eye and a
lump the size of a pullet egg swelling above his
ear.

"Aha!" he yelled. "Right under my roof, you
Jezebel!"

"Your roof!" Swinehild yelled back, as O'Leary

recoiled against the wall. "My old man left the dump to me, as I remember, and out of the goodness of my heart I took you in off the streets after the monkey ran away with your grind-organ or whatever that hard-luck story you gave me was!"

"I knew the second I set eyes on this slicked-up fancy-dancer, you and him had something cooking!" Hulk countered, aiming a finger like a horse pistol at O'Leary. He jammed the lantern on a hook by the door, pushed his sleeves up past biceps like summer squashes, and dived across the bed. Lafayette, with a desperate lunge, tore free of the confining coverlet and slipped down between the mattress and the wall. The impact as Hulk's head met the plaster was reminiscent of that produced by an enraged *toro* charging the *barrera*. The big man rebounded and slid to the floor like a two-hundred-pound bag of canned goods.

"Say, you've got quite a punch, Lafe," Swinehild said admiringly from somewhere above Lafayette. "He had it coming to him, the big side of beef!"

Lafayette, his arms and legs entangled in apparently endless swathes of blanket, fought his way clear, emerged from under the bed, to meet Swinehild's eyes peering down at him.

"You're a funny guy," she said. "First you knock him cold with one sock, and then you hide under the bed."

"I was just looking around for my contact lenses," Lafayette said haughtily, rising. "But never mind. I only need them for close work like writing my will." He grabbed for his clothes, began pulling them on at top speed.

"I guess you got the right idea at that," Swinehild sighed, tossing a lock of palest blond hair back over a shapely shoulder. "When Hulk wakes up, he's not going to be in his best mood." She sorted through the disarranged bedding for her clothes, began donning them.

"That's all right, you don't need to see me off," Lafayette said hastily. "I know the way."

"See you off? Are you kidding, Jack? You think I'm going to hang around here after this? Let's get out of here before he comes to, roaring, and you have to belt him again."

"Well—I suppose it might be a good idea if you went and stayed with your mother until Hulk cools down a little, so that you can explain that it wasn't what it looked like."

"It wasn't?" Swinehild looked puzzled. "Then what was it? But never mind answering. You're a funny guy, Lafe, but I guess you mean well—which is more than you could say for Hulk, the big baboon!" Lafayette thought he saw the gleam of a tear at the corner of one blue eye, but she turned away before he could be sure.

Swinehild did up the buttons on her bodice, pulled open the door to a rackety clothes press behind the door, and took out a heavy cloak.

"I'll just make up a snack to take along," she said, slipping out into the dark hall. Lafayette followed with the lantern. In the kitchen he stood by restlessly, shifting from one foot to the other and listening intently for sounds from upstairs while Swinehild packed a basket with a loaf of coarse bread, a link of blackish sausage, apples, and yellow cheese, added a paring knife and a hand-blown bottle of a dubious-looking purplish wine.

"That's very thoughtful of you," Lafayette said, taking the basket. "I hope you'll allow me to offer a small additional token of my esteem."

"Keep it," Swinehild said as he dug into his pocket. "We'll need it on the trip."

"We?" Lafayette's eyebrows went up. "How far away does your mother live?"

"What have you got, one of them mother fixations? My old lady died when I was a year old. Let's dust, Lafe. We've got ground to cover before himself gets on our trail." She pulled open the back door, allowing ingress to a gust of chill night air.

"B-but you can't come with me!"

"Why can't I? We're going to the same place."

"You want to see the duke too? I thought you said—"

"A pox on the duke! I just want to get to the big town, see the bright lights, get in on a little action before I'm too old. I've spent the best years o' my life washing out that big elephant's socks after I took 'em off him by force—and what do I get for it? A swell right-arm action from swinging a skillet in self-defense!"

"But—what will people think? I mean, Hulk isn't likely to understand that I have no interest in you—I mean no improper interest—"

Swinehild lifted her chin and thrust out her lower lip defiantly—an expression with which Princess Adoranne had broken hearts in job lots.

"My mistake, noble sir. Now that you mention it, I guess I'd slow you down. You go ahead. I'll make it on my own." She turned and strode off along the moon-bright street. This time O'Leary was sure he saw a tear wink on her cheek.

"Swinehild, wait!" He dashed after her, plucked at her cloak. "I meant—I didn't mean—"

"Skip it, if you don't mind," she said in a voice in which Lafayette detected a slight break, ruthlessly suppressed. "I got by O.K. before you showed up, and I'll get by after you're gone."

"Swinehild, to tell you the truth," O'Leary blurted, trotting beside her, "the reason I was, ah, hesitant about our traveling together was that I, ah, feel such a powerful attraction for you. I mean, I'm not sure I could promise to be a perfect gentleman at all times, and me being a married man, and you a married woman, and . . . and . . ." He paused to gulp air as Swinehild turned, looked searchingly into his face, then smiled brilliantly and threw her arms around his neck. Her velvet-smooth lips pressed hard against his; her admirable contours nestled against him. . . .

"I was afraid I was losing my stuff," she confided, nibbling his ear. "You're a funny one, Lafe. But I guess it's just because you're such a gent, like you said, that you think you have to insult a girl."

"That's it exactly," Lafayette agreed hurriedly. "That and the thought of what my wife and your husband would say."

"If that's all that's worrying you, forget it." Swinehild tossed her head. "Come on; if we stretch a leg, we can be in Port Miasma by cockcrow."

Three

Topping a low rise of stony ground, Lafayette looked down across a long slope of arid, moonlit countryside to the silvered expanse of a broad lake that stretched out to a horizon lost in distance, its smooth surface broken by a chain of islands that marched in a long curve that was an extension of the row of hills to his left. On the last island in line, the lights of a town sparkled hidtantly.

"It's hard to believe I made a hike across that same stretch of country once," he said. "If I hadn't found an oasis with a Coke machine, I'd have ended up a set of dry bones."

"My feet hurt," Swinehild groaned. "Let's take ten."

They settled themselves on the ground and O'Leary opened the lunch basket, from which a powerful aroma of garlic arose. He carved slices of sausage, and they chewed, looking up at the stars.

"Funny," Swinehild said. "When I was a kid, I used to imagine there was people on all those stars out there. They all lived in beautiful gardens and danced and played all day long. I had an idea I was an orphan, marooned from someplace like that, and that someday my real folks would come along and take me back."

"The curious thing about me," Lafayette said, "was that I didn't think anything like that at all. And then one day I discovered that all I had to do was focus my psychic energies, and zap! There I was in Artesia."

"Look, Lafe," Swinehild said, "you're too nice a guy to go around talking like a nut. It's one thing to dream pretty dreams, but it's something else when you start believing 'em. Why don't you forget all this sidekick-energy stuff and just face facts: you're stuck in humdrum old Melange, like it or not. It ain't much, but it's real."

"Artesia," Lafayette murmured. "I could have been king there—only I turned it down. Too demanding. But you were a princess, Swinehild. And Hulk was a count. A marvelous fellow, once you got to know him—"

"Me, a princess?" Swinehild laughed, not very merrily. "I'm a kitchen slavey, Lafe. It's all I'm cut out for. Can you picture me all dolled up in a fancy gown, snooting everybody and leading a poodle around on a leash?"

"A tiger cub," Lafayette corrected. "And you didn't snoot people; you had a perfectly charming personality. Of course you did get a little huffy once, when you thought I'd invited a chambermaid to the big dance—"

"Well, sure, why not?" Swinechild said. "If I was throwing a big shindig, I wouldn't want any grubby little serving wenches lousing up the atmosphere, would I?"

"Just a minute," O'Leary came back hotly.

"Daphne was as pretty and sweet as any girl at the ball—except maybe you. All she needed to shine was a good bath and a nice dress."

"It would take more'n a new set of duds to make a lady out o' me," Swinehild said complacently.

"Nonsense," Lafayette contradicted. "If you just made a little effort, you could be as good as anyone—or better!"

"You think if I dress fancy and tiptoe around not getting my hands dirty, that'll make me any better than what I am?"

"That's not what I meant. I just meant—"

"Never mind, Lafe. The conversation is getting too deep. I got a nice little body on me, and I'm strong and willing. If I can't get by on that, to perdition with the lace pants, get me?"

"I'll tell you what: when we get to the capital, we'll go and have your hair done, and—"

"My hair's Jake with me like it is. Skip it, Lafe. Let's get moving. We still got a long way to go before we can flop—and getting across that lake won't be no picnic."

The lake shore in the lee of the rocky headland was marshy, odiferous of mud and rotted vegetation and expired fish. Lafayette and Swinehild stood shivering in ankle-deep muck, scanning the dark-curving strand for signs of commercial transportation facilities to ferry them out to the island city, the lights of which winked and sparkled cheerfully across the black waters.

"I guess the old tub sank," Swinehild said. "Used to be it ran out to the city every hour on the hour, a buck-fifty one way."

"It looks like we'll have to find an alternate

mode of travel," O'Leary commented. "Come on. These huts along the shore are probably fishermen's shacks. We ought to be able to hire a man to row us out."

"I ought to warn you, Lafe, these fishermen got a kind of unsavory rep. Like as not they'd tap you over the head and clean out your pockets, and throw the remains in the lake."

"That's a chance we'll have to take. We can't stay here freezing to death."

"Listen, Lafe—" She caught at his arm. "Let's just scout along the shore and find us a rowboat that ain't tied down too good, and—"

"You mean steal some poor fellow's means of livelihood? Swinehild, I'm ashamed of you!"

"O.K., you wait here and *I'll* take care of getting the boat."

"Your attitude does you no credit, Swinehild," Lafayette said sternly. "We'll go about this in a straightforward, aboveboard manner. Honesty is the best policy, remember that."

"You sure got some funny ideas, Lafe. But it's your neck."

He led the way across the mud to the nearest shack, a falling-down structure of water-rotted boards with a rusted stovepipe poking out the side, from which a meager coil of smoke shredded into the brisk, icy wind. A faint gleam of light shone under the single boarded-up window. Lafayette rapped at the door. After a pause, bedsprings creaked inside.

"Yeah?" a hoarse voice responded without enthusiasm.

"Ah—we're a couple of travelers," Lafayette called. "We need transportation out to the capital.

We're prepared to pay well—" he *oof!*ed as Swinehild's elbow drove into his side. "As well as we can, that is."

Muttering was audible, accompanied by the sound of a bolt being withdrawn. The door opened six inches, and a bleary, red-rimmed eye under a shaggy eyebrow peered forth at shoulder level.

"What are youse?" the voice that went with the eye said. "Nuts or something?"

"Mind your tone," Lafayette said sharply. "There's a lady present."

The bleary eye probed past O'Leary at Swinehild. The wide mouth visible below the eye stretched in a grin that revealed a surprising number of large, carious teeth.

"Whyncha say so, sport? That's different." The eye tracked appreciatively down, paused, up again. "Yeah, not bad at all. What did you say youse wanted, squire?"

"We have to get to Port Miasma," Lafayette said, sidling over to block the cabin dweller's view of Swinehild. "It's a matter of vast importance."

"Yeah. Well, in the morning—"

"We can't wait until morning," Lafayette cut in. "Aside from the fact that we have no intention of spending the night on this mud flat, it's essential that we get away—I mean reach the capital without delay."

"Well—I'll tell you what I'll do; outa the goodness of my heart I'll let the little lady spend the night inside. I'll throw you out a tarp, cap'n, to keep the wind off, and in the A.M.—"

"You don't seem to understand!" O'Leary cut in. "We want to go now—at once—immediately."

"Uh-huh," the native said, covering a cavernous yawn with a large-knuckled hand matted on the back with dense black hairs. "Well, Cull, what youse need is a boat—"

"Look here," O'Leary snapped. "I'm standing out here in the cold wind offering you this"—he reached in his pocket and produced a second Artesian fifty-cent piece—"to ferry us out there! Are you interested, or aren't you?"

"Hey!" the man said. "That looks like solid silver."

"Naturally," Lafayette said. "Do you want it or don't you?"

"Geeze, thanks, bub—" The knuckly hand reached, but Lafayette snatched the coin back.

"Ah-ah," he reproved. "First you have to row us out to the city."

"Yeah." The hand went up to scratch at a rumpled head of coarse black hair with a sound like a carpenter filing a knot. "There's just one small problem area there, yer lordship. But maybe I got a solution," he added more briskly. "But the price will be the silver piece plus a sample o' the little lady's favors. I'll take a little o' that last on account." The hand poked at O'Leary as if to brush him aside. He gave it a sharp rap on the knuckles, at which the owner jerked it back and popped the wounded members into his mouth.

"Ouch!" he said, looking up at O'Leary reproachfully. "That hurt, guy!"

"It was meant to," Lafayette said coldly. "If I weren't in such a hurry, I'd haul you out of there and give you a sound thrashing!"

"Yeah? Well, you might run into a little trouble there, chief. I'm kind of a heavy guy to haul around." There was a stir, and the head thrust through the door, followed by a pair of shoulders no wider than a hay rick, a massive torso; on all fours, the owner of the hut emerged, climbed to a pair of feet the size of skate boards, and stood, towering a good seven-foot-six into the damp night air.

"So O.K., I'll wait and collect at the other end," the monster said. "Prob'ly a good idea if I work up a good sweat first anyway. Wait here. I'll be back in short order."

"I got to hand it to you, Lafe," Swinehild murmured as the giant strode away into the mist. "You don't let a little beef scare you." She looked lingeringly after the big man. "Not that he don't have a certain animal charm," she added.

"If he lays a hand on you, I'll tear his head off and stuff it down his throat!" Lafayette snapped.

"Hey, Lafe—you're jealous!" Swinehild said delightedly. "But don't let it get out of hand," she added. "I had enough of getting backhanded ears over teakettle every time some bum looks over my architecture."

"Jealous? Me? You're out of your mind." O'Leary jammed his hands in his pockets and began pacing up and down, while Swinehild hummed softly to herself and twiddled with her hair.

It was the better part of a quarter of an hour before the big man returned, moving with surprising softness for his bulk.

"All set," he called in a hoarse whisper. "Let's go."

"What's all the creeping around and whispering for?" O'Leary demanded loudly. "What—"

With a swift move, the giant clapped a hand as
hard as saddle leather across his mouth.

"Keep it down, Bo," he hissed. "We don't want
to wake the neighbors. The boys need their sleep,
the hours they work."

O'Leary squirmed free of the grip, snorting a
sharp odor of tar and herring from his nostrils.

"Well, naturally, I don't want to commit a nuisance," he whispered. He took Swinehild's hand,
led her in the wake of their guide down across the
mucky beach to a crumbling stone jetty at the end
of which a clumsy, flat-bottomed dory was tied
up. It settled six inches lower in the water as the
big man climbed in and settled himself on the
rowing bench. Lafayette handed Swinehild
down, gritting his teeth as the boatman picked her
up by the waist and lifted her past him to the stern
seat.

"You sit in the front, bub, and watch for floating
logs," the big man said. Lafayette was barely in
his place when the oars dipped in and sent the
boat off with a surge that almost tipped him over
the side. He hung on grimly, listening to the creak
of the oarlocks, the splash of small waves under
the bow, watching the dock recede swiftly, to
disappear into the gathering mist. Twisting to
look over his shoulder, he saw the distant city
lights, haloed by fog, floating far away across the
choppy black water. The damp wind seemed to
penetrate his bones.

"How long will the trip take?" he called
hoarsely, hugging himself.

"Shhh," the oarsman hissed over his shoulder.

"What's the matter now? Are you afraid you'll
wake up the fish?" Lafayette snapped.

"Have a heart, pal," the big man whispered urgently. "Sound carries over water like nobody's business. . . ." He cocked his head as if listening. Faintly, from the direction of the shore, Lafayette heard a shout.

"Well, it seems everybody isn't as scrupulous as we are," he said tartly. "Is it all right if we talk now? Or—"

"Can it, Buster!" the giant hissed. "They'll hear us!"

"Who?" Lafayette inquired loudly. "What's going on here? Why are we acting like fugitives?"

"On account of the guy I borrowed the boat from might not like the idea too good," the giant rumbled. "But I guess the fat's on the hotplate now. Some o' them guys got ears like bats."

"What idea might the fellow you borrowed the boat from not like?" Lafayette inquired in a puzzled tone.

"The idea I borrowed the boat."

"You mean you didn't have his permission?"

"I hate to wake a guy outa a sound sleep wit' a like frivolous request."

"Why, you . . . you . . ."

"Just call me Clutch, bub. Save the fancy names for the bums which are now undoubtedly pushing off in pursuit." Clutch bent his back to the oars, sending the boat leaping ahead.

"Great," Lafayette groaned. "Perfect. This is our reward for being honest: a race through the night with the police baying on our trail!"

"I'll level wit' youse," Clutch said. "These boys ain't no cops. And they ain't got what you'd call a whole lot o' inhibitions. If they catch us, what they'll hand us won't be no subpoena."

"Look," Lafayette said quickly, "we'll turn back, and explain that the whole thing was a misunderstanding—"

"Maybe you like the idea o' being fed to the fish, yer worship, but not me," Clutch stated. "And we got the little lady to think of, too. Them boys is a long time between gals."

"Don't waste breath," Lafayette said. "Save it for rowing."

"If I row any harder, the oars'll bust," Clutch said. "Sounds like they're gaining on us, Cull. Looks like I'll have to lighten ship."

"Good idea," Lafayette agreed. "What can we throw overboard?"

"Well, there ain't no loose gear to jettison; and I got to stick wit' the craft in order to I should row. And naturally we can't toss the little lady over the side, except as a last resort, like. So I guess that leaves you, chum."

"Me?" Lafayette echoed. "Look here, Clutch— I'm the one who hired you, remember? You can't be serious—"

"Afraid so, Mac." The big man shipped oars, dusted his hands, and turned on his bench.

"But—who's going to pay you, if I'm in the lake?" O'Leary temporized, retreating to the farthermost angle of the bows.

"Yeah—there is that," Clutch agreed, stroking his Gibraltarlike chin. "Maybe you better hand over the poke first."

"Not a chance. If I go, it goes!"

"Well—I guess we ain't got room to like scuffle. So—since youse want to be petty about it, I'll just have to collect double from the little lady." Clutch rose in a smooth lunge, one massive arm reaching for Lafayette. The latter ducked under the closing hand and launched himself in a headfirst dive at the other's midriff, instead crashed into a brick wall that had suddenly replaced it. As he clawed at the floorboards, he was dimly aware of a swishing sound, a solid *thud!* as of a mallet striking a tent stake, followed a moment later by a marine earthquake which tossed the boat like a juggler's egg. A faceful of icy water brought him upright, striking out gamely.

"Easy, Lafe," Swinehild called. "I clipped him with the oar and he landed on his chin. Damn near swamped us. We better get him over the side fast."

Lafayette focused his eyes with difficulty, made out the inert form of the giant draped face down across the gunwale, one oak-root arm trailing in the water.

"We . . . we can't do that," Lafayette gasped. "He's unconscious; he'd drown." He took the oar from her, groped his way to the rover's bench, thrust Clutch's elephantine leg aside, dipped in, and pulled—

The oar snapped with a sharp report, sending Lafayette in a forward dive into the scuppers.

"I guess I swung it too hard," Swinehild said regretfully. "It's all that skillet-work done it."

Lafayette scrabbled back to the bench, ignoring the shooting pains in his head, neck, eyeballs, and elsewhere. "I'll have to scull with one oar," he panted. "Which direction?"

"Dunno," Swinehild said. "But I guess it don't matter much. Look."

O'Leary followed her pointing finger. A ghostly

white patch, roughly triangular in shape, loomed off the port bow, rushing toward them out of the dense fog.

"It's a sailboat," Lafayette gasped as the pursuer hove into full view, cleaving the mist. He could see half a dozen men crouched on the deck of the vessel. They raised a shout as they saw the drift-ing rowboat, changed course to sweep up alongside. Lafayette shattered the remaining oar over the head of the first of the boarders to leap the rail, before an iceberg he had failed to notice until that moment fell on him, burying him under a hundred tons of boulders and frozen mammoth bones. . . .

O'Leary regained consciousness standing on his face in half an inch of iced cabbage broth with a temple gong echoing in his skull. The floor under him was rising up and up and over in a never-ending loop-the-loop, but when he at-tempted to clutch for support he discovered that both arms had been lopped off at the shoulder. He worked his legs, succeeded in driving his face farther into the bilge, which sloshed and gurgled merrily down between his collar and his neck before draining away with the next tilt of the deck. He threshed harder, flopped over on his back, and blinked his eyes clear. He was lying, it appeared, in the cockpit of the small sailing craft. His arms had not been amputated after all, he discovered as fiery pains lanced out from his tightly bound wrists.

"Hey, Fancy-pants is awake," a cheery voice called. "O.K. if I step on his mush a couple times?"

"Wait until we get through drawing straws fer the wench."

O'Leary shook his head, sending a whole new lexicon of aches swirling through it, but clearing his vision slightly. Half a dozen pairs of burly rubber-booted legs were grouped around the binnacle light, matching the burly bodies looming above them. Swinehild, standing by with her arms held behind her by a pock-marked man with a notched ear, drove a sudden kick into a handy shin. The recipient of the attention leaped and swore, while his fellows guffawed in hearty good fellowship.

"She's a lively 'un," a toothless fellow with greasy, shoulder-length hair stated. "Who's got the straws?"

"Ain't no straws aboard," another stated. "We'll have to use fish."

"I dunno," demurred a short, wide fellow with a blue-black beard which all but enveloped his eyes. "Never heard of drawing fish for a wench. We want to do this right, according to the rules and all."

"Skip the seafood, boys," Swinehild suggested. "I kind of got a habit of picking my own boyfriends. Now you, good-looking . . ." She gave a saucy glance to the biggest of the crew, a lantern-jawed chap with a sheaf of stiff wheat-colored hair and a porridgy complexion. "You're more my style. You going to let these rag-pickers come between us?"

The one thus singled out gaped, grinned, flexed massive, crooked shoulders, and threw out his chest.

"Well, boys, I guess that settles that—"

A marlinspike wielded by an unidentified hand described a short arc ending alongside the lantern jaw, the owner of which did a half-spin and sank out of sight.

"None o' that, wench," a gruff voice commanded. "Don't go trying to stir up no dissension. With us, it's share and share alike. Right, boys?"

As a chorus of assent rang out, Lafayette struggled to a sitting position, cracking his head on the tiller just above him. It was unattended, lashed in position, holding the craft on a sharply heeled into-the-wind course, the boom-mounted sail bellying tautly above the frothing waves. O'Leary tugged at his bonds; the ropes cutting into his wrists were as unyielding as cast-iron manacles. The crewmen were laughing merrily at a coarse jape, ogling Swinehild, while one of their number adjusted a row of kippered herring in his hand, his tongue protruding from the corner of his mouth with the intensity of his concentration. The object of the lottery stood, her wet garments plastered against her trim figure, her chin high, her lips blue with cold.

O'Leary groaned silently. A fine protector for a girl he'd turned out to be. If he hadn't pigheadedly insisted on doing things his own way, they'd never have gotten into this spot. And this was one mess from which he was unlikely to emerge alive. Swinehild had warned him the locals would cheerfully feed him to the fish. Probably they were keeping him alive until they could get around to robbing him of everything, including the clothes on his back, and then over he'd go, with or without a knife between the ribs. And Swinehild, poor creature—her dream of making it big in the big town would end right here with this crew of cutthroats. Lafayette twisted savagely at his bonds. If he could get one hand free; if he could just take one of these grinning apes to the bottom with him; if he only had one small remaining flicker of his old power over the psychic energies . . .

Lafayette drew a calming breath and forced himself to relax. No point in banging his head on any more stone walls. He couldn't break half-inch hemp ropes with his bare hands. But if he could, somehow, manage just one little miracle— nothing to compare with shifting himself to Artesia, of course, or summoning up a dragon on order, or even supplying himself with a box of Aunt Hooty's taffies on demand. He'd settle for just one tiny rearrangement of the situation, something—anything at all to give him a chance.

"That's all I ask," he murmured, squeezing his eyes shut. "Just a chance." *But I've got to be specific,* he reminded himself. *Focusing the psychic energies isn't magic, after all. It's just a matter of drawing on the entropic energy of the universe to manipulate things into a configuration nearer to my heart's desire. Like, for example, if the ropes were to be loose . . .*

"But they aren't loose," he told himslf sternly. "You can't change any known element of the situation. At best, you can influence what happens next, that's all. And probably not even that."

Well, then—if there was a knife lying here on deck—an old rusty scaling knife, say, just carelessly tossed aside. I could get my hands on it, and—

"Lay down and sleep it off, landlubber," a voice

boomed, accompanying the suggestion with a kick on the ear that produced a shower of small ringed planets whirling in a mad dance. Lafayette blinked them away, snorted a sharp aroma of aged cheese and garlic from his nostrils. Something with the texture of barbed wire was rasping the side of his neck. He twisted away from it, felt something round rolling under him. An apple, he realized as it crunched, releasing a fresh fruity odor. And the cheese and the sausage . . .

He held his breath. It was the lunch basket. The pirates had tossed it aboard along with the prisoners. And in the basket there had been a knife.

Lafayette opened one eye and checked the positions of his captors. Four of them stood heads together, intently studying the array of fishheads offered by the fifth. The sixth man lay snoring at their feet. Swinehild was huddled on the deck—knocked there by one of her would-be swains, no doubt.

Cautiously, O'Leary fingered the deck under him with his bound hands; inching sideways, he encountered the loaf of bread, reduced by soaking to a sodden paste, then a second apple, flattened by a boot. He reached the basket, felt over it, found it empty. The sausage lay half under it. Lafayette hitched himself forward another six inches, grinding the cheese under his shoulderblades. As the waves thumped the hull under him, his numb fingers closed over the haft of the knife.

It was small, the blade no more than four inches long—but it was big enough for his purpose. The crewmen were still busy with their lottery. Lafayette rolled over, struggled to his knees, maneuvered into position with his back against the tiller. Gripping the knife, he felt for the lashings, began sawing through the twisted rope.

It was an agonizing two minutes before a sharp, musical *thong!* sounded; the suddenly freed tiller gouged Lafayette painfully in the ribs as it slammed around to a full starboard position. Instantly the boat heeled sharply, falling away downwind. The crewmen, caught by surprise, reeled against the rail, grabbing for support. The boat gave a wild plunge, the sail slatting as the breeze struck it dead astern. Cordage creaked; the sail bulged, then, with a report like a pistol shot, filled. The boom swept across the deck—precisely at head height, Lafayette noted, as it gathered in the four sailors and sent them flying over the side, where they struck with a tremendous quadruple splash as the pilotless craft went leaping ahead across the dark water.

Four

"Your poor head," Swinehild said, applying a cool compress made from a section of her skirt to one of the knots on O'Leary's skull. "Them boys throwed you around like a sack o'turnips."

"My ear feels the size of a baked potato, and about the same temperature," Lafayette said. "Not that I suppose it actually gleams in the dark." He peered across toward the misty glow in the middle distance toward which he was steering.

"In a way those hijackers did us a favor," he commented. "We'd never have made such good time rowing."

"You got kind of a irritating way o' looking on the bright side, Lafe," Swinehild sighed. "I wish you'd work on that."

"Now, Swinehild, this is no time to be discouraged." Lafayette jollied her. "True, we're cold and wet and so tired we ache all over; but the worst is over. We got out of an extremely tight spot with no more than a few bruises to my head and your dignity. In a few minutes we'll be tucking our feet under a table for a bowl of hot soup and a little drop of something to cut the chill, and then off to the best hotel in town."

"Sure, it's OK for you to talk. With that slick

line o' chatter o' yours, you'll probably land a swell job with the duke, soothsaying or something."

"I don't want a job," Lafayette pointed out. "I just want to get out of Melange and back to the comfortable monotony I was fool enough to complain about a few hours ago."

O'Leary brought the boat smartly about on the starboard tack, closing in on the ever-widening spread of city lights ahead. They passed a bell-buoy dinging lonesomely in the mist, sailed past a shore lined with high-fronted buildings recalling the waterfront at Amsterdam, backed by rising tiers of houses clustered about the base of a massive keep of lead-colored granite, approached a lighted loading dock where a number of nondescript small craft were tied up, bobbing gently on the waves. As they came alongside, Swinehild threw a line to an urchin, who hauled it in and made it fast. Flickering gas lights on the quay above shed a queasy light on wet cobbles well strewn with refuse. A couple of dockside loafers watched incuriously as Lafayette assisted Swinehild from the boat, tossing a nickel to the lad. A stray dog with a down-curled tail slunk away past the darkened fronts of the marine-supply houses across the way as they started across the cobbles.

"Geeze—the big town," Swinehild said reverently, brushing a curl from her eyes. "Port Miasma—and it's even bigger and glamorouser than I expected."

"Um," Lafayette said noncommittally, leading the way toward the lighted entry of a down-at-heels grog shop just visible at an angle halfway up a steep side street, before which a weathered board announced YE GUT BUCKET.

Inside the smoky but warm room, they took a corner table. The sleepy-eyed tavern-keeper silently accepted their order and shuffled away.

"Well, this is more like it," Lafayette said with a sigh. "It's been a strenuous night, but with a hot meal and a good bed to look forward to, we can't complain."

"The big town scares me, Lafe," Swinehild said. "It's so kind of impersonal, all hustle-bustle, no time for them little personal touches that mean so much to a body."

"Hustle-bustle? It's as dead as a foreclosed mortuary," Lafayette muttered.

"Like this place," Swinehild continued. "Open in the middle o' the night. Never seen anything like it."

"It's hardly ten P.M.," Lafayette pointed out. "And—"

"And besides that, I got to go," Swinehild added. "And not a clump o' bushes in sight."

"There's a room for it," O'Leary said hastily. "Over there—where it says LADIES."

"You mean—*inside?*"

"Of course. You're in town now, Swinehild. You have to start getting used to a few amenities—"

"Never mind; I'll just duck out in the alley—"

"Swinehild! The ladies' room, please!"

"You come with me."

"I can't—it's for ladies only. There's another one for men."

"Well, think o' that!" Swinehild shook her head wonderingly.

"Now hurry along, our soup will be here in a minute."

"Wish me luck." Swinehild rose and moved off hesitantly. Lafayette sighed, turned back the soggy lace from his wrists, used the worn napkin beside his plate to mop the condensed moisture from his face, sniffing the bouquet of chicken and onions drifting in from the kitchen. His mouth watered at the prospect. Except for a chunk of salami, and that plate of dubious pork back at the Beggar's Bole, he hadn't eaten a bite since lunch . . .

Lunch, ten hours and a million years ago: the dainty table set up on the terrace, the snowy linen, the polished silver, the deft *sommelier* pouring the feather-light wine from the frosted and napkin-wrapped bottle, the delicate slices of savory ham, the angelfood cake with whipped cream, the paper-thin cup of steaming coffee—

"Hey—you!" a deep voice boomed across the room, shattering O'Leary's reverie. He looked around to see who was thus rudely addressed, saw a pair of tall fellows in gold-braided blue tailcoats, white knee breeches, buckled shoes, and tricorner hats bearing down on him from the door.

"Yeah—it's him," the smaller of the two said, grabbing for his sword hilt. "Boy oh boy, the pinch of the week, and it's ours, all ours, Snardley—so don't louse it up." The rapier cleared its sheath with a whistling rasp. Its owner waved it at O'Leary.

"Hold it right there, pal," he said in a flinty voice. "You're under arrest in the name of the duke!"

The second uniformed man had drawn a long-muzzled flintlock pistol of the type associated with Long John Silver; he flourished it in a careless manner at O'Leary's head.

"You going in quiet, rube, or have I gotta plug you, resisting arrest?"

"You've got the wrong rube," Lafayette replied impatiently. "I just arrived: I haven't had time to break any laws—unless you've got one against breathing."

"Not yet—but it's a thought, wise guy." The rapier-wielder jabbed sharply at him. "Better come along nice, Bo: Yockwell and me collect the same reward, dead or alive."

"I seen what you taken and done to a couple pals of mine, which they was snuck up on from behind," Yockwell warned. "I'm just itching for a excuse to get even." He thumbed back the hammer of the big pistol with an ominous click.

"You're out of your minds!" O'Leary protested. "I've never been to this water-logged slum before in my life!"

"Tell it to Duke Rodolpho." The sword poked Lafayette painfully. "Pick 'em up, Dude. We got a short walk ahead."

O'Leary glanced toward the ladies' room as he got to his feet: the door was closed and silent. The landlord stood furtive-eyed behind the bar, polishing a pewter tankard. Lafayette caught his eye, mouthed an urgent message. The man blinked and made a sign as if warding off the evil eye.

"You fellows are making a big mistake," Lafayette said as a push helped him toward the door. "Probably right now the man you're really

after is making a fast getaway. Your bosses aren't
going to like it—"

"You either, chum. Now button the chin."

A few furtive passersby gaped as the two cops
herded O'Leary up the narrow, crooked street
which wound sharply toward the grim pile towering over the town. They passed through a high
iron gate guarded by a pair of sentries in uniforms
like those of the arresting patrolmen, crossed a
cobbled courtyard to a wooden door flanked by
smoking flambeaux. It opened on a bright-lit
room with hand-drawn WANTED posters on the
walls, a wooden bench, a table stacked with
curled papers in dusty bundles.

"Well, look who's here," a lean fellow with a
yellowish complexion said, picking up a bedraggled quill and pulling a blank form toward him.
"You made a mistake coming back, smart guy."

"Coming back wh—" A sharp jab in the back
cut off O'Leary's objections. His captors grabbed
his arms, hustled him through an iron-barred
door and along a dark passage ending in a flight of
steps that led downward into an odor like the
gorilla house at the St. Louis zoo.

"Oh, no," Lafayette protested, digging in his
heels. "You're not taking me down there!"

"Right," Yockwell confirmed. "See you later,
joker!" A foot in the seat propelled Lafayette forward; he half-leaped, half-fell down the steps,
landed in a heap in a low-ceilinged chamber lit by
a single tallow candle and lined with barred cages
from which shaggy, animal-like faces leered. At
one side of the room a man wider than his height

sat on a three-legged stool paring his nails with a sixteen-inch Bowie knife.

"Welcome to the group," the attendant called in a tone like a meat grinder gnawing through gristle. "Lucky fer you, we got a vacancy."

Lafayette leaped to his feet and made three steps before an iron grille crashed down across the steps, barely missing his toes.

"Close," the receptionist said. "Another six inches and I'd of been mopping brains off the floor."

"What's this all about?" Lafayette inquired in a broken voice.

"Easy," the jailer said, jangling keys. "You're back in stir, and this time you don't sneak out when I ain't looking."

"I demand a lawyer. I don't know what I'm accused of, but whatever it is, I'm innocent!"

"You never hit no guys over the head?" The jailer wrinkled his forehead in mock surprise.

"Well, as to that—"

"You never croaked nobody?"

"Not intentionally. You see—"

"Never conspired at a little larceny? Never wandered into the wrong bedroom by mistake?"

"I can explain—" Lafayette cried.

"Skip it," the turnkey yawned, selecting a key from the ring. "We already had the trial. You're guilty on all counts. Better relax and grab a few hours' sleep, so's you'll be in shape for the big day tomorrow."

"Tomorrow? What happens tomorrow?"

"Nothing much." The jailer grabbed Lafayette

by the collar of his bedraggled plum coat and hustled him into a cell. "Just a small beheading at dawn, with you as the main attraction."

Lafayette huddled in the corner of the cramped cell, doing his best to ignore his various aches and pains, the itching occasioned by the insect life that shared his accommodations, the mice that ran across his feet, the thick, fudgy odor, and the deep, glottal snores of the other inmates. He also tried, with less success, to keep his mind off the grisly event scheduled for the next morning.

"Poor Swinehild," he muttered to his knees. "She'll think I ran off and deserted her. She'll never trust another ladies' room as long as she lives. Poor kid, alone in this miserable imitation of a medieval hell-town, with no money, no friends, no place to lay her head. . . ."

"Hey, Lafe," a familiar voice hissed from the murk behind him. "This way. We got about six minutes to make it back up to the postern gate before the night watchman makes his next round!"

"Swinehild," Lafayette mumbled, gaping at the tousled blond head poking through the rectangular aperture in the back wall of the cell. "Where did you—how—what—?"

"Shh! You'll wake up the screw!" Lafayette glanced across toward the guard. He sat slumped on his stool like a dreaming Buddha, his fingers interlaced across his paunch, his head resting comfortably against the wall.

"I'll hafta back out," Swinehild said. "Come on; it's a long crawl." Her face disappeared. Lafayette tottered to his feet, started into the hole head first.

It was a roughly mortared tunnel barely big enough to admit him. A cold draft blew through it.

"Put the stone back," Swinehild hissed.

"How? With my feet?"

"Well—let it go. Maybe nobody'll notice it for a while in that light."

His face bumped hers in the darkness; her lips nibbled his cheek. She giggled.

"If you don't beat all, Lafe, grabbing a smooch at a time like this. Anybody else'd be thinking o' nothing but putting distance between hisself and that basket party."

"How did you find out where I was?" Lafayette inquired, scrambling after her as she retreated.

"The tapman told me they'd put the sneeze on you. I followed along to the gate and made friends with the boys there. One of 'em let slip about this back way in. Seems like another feller escaped the same way, just a couple days back."

"They told you all that, on such short acquaintance?"

"Well, look at it their way, Lafe: low pay, long hours—and what's it to them if some poor sucker Rodolpho's got it in for cheats the headsman?"

"Well, that was certainly friendly of them."

"Yeah, but it was kinda tough on my back. Boy, them cold stone floors them boys has to stand on!"

"Swinehild—you don't mean—but never mind," Lafayette hurried on. "I'd rather not have it confirmed."

"Careful, now," Swinehild cautioned. "We go up a steep slant here and come out under a juniper bush. Just outside there's a guy pounding a beat."

Using elbows, toes, and fingernails, Lafayette

crept up the incline. A the top, he waited while Swinehild listened.

"Here goes," she said. There was a soft creak, and dim light filtered in, along with a wisp of fog. A moment later, they were across the alley and over a low wall into a small park. They picked their way among trees and shrubs to a secluded spot in the center of a dense clump of myrtle.

"And I was worried about you," Lafayette said, flopping down on the ground. "Swinehild, it's a miracle; I still don't believe it. If it weren't for you, in another three hours I'd have been shorter by a head."

"And if it wasn't for you, I'd still be playing ring-around-the-rosy with them five deck-apes, Lafe." She snuggled close to him on the carpet of fragrant leaves.

"Yes, but it was me that got you into the situation in the first place, dragging you off in the middle of the night—"

"Yeah, but I was the one got you in bad with Hulk. He ain't really such a bad guy, but he ain't long on brains, always jumping to conclusions. Why, if he was to come along now, I bet the dummy'd try to make something of you and me here in the bushes together!"

"Er, yes." Lafayette edged away from the warm body beside him. "But right now we have to give some thought to our next move. I can't show my face around this place; either they've mistaken me for someone else, or those sailors we ditched are the world's fastest swimmers."

"We never did get nothing to eat," Swinehild said. "Or did they feed you in jail?"

"It must have been the caterer's day off,"

O'Leary said sadly. "I'd even welcome another slice of that leatherwurst we had in our lunch basket."

"You peeked," Swinehild said, and produced the sausage from a capacious reticule, along with the paring knife and the villainous-looking vintage Lafayette had last seen sliding about the bilge of the sailboat.

"Clever girl," Lafayette breathed. He used the knife to cut thick slices of the garlicky sausage, halved the apple, and dug the cork from the bottle.

"Nothing like a picnic under the stars," he said, chewing doggedly at the tough meat.

"Gee, this is the kind o' life I always pictured," Swinehild said, closing the distance between them and sliding her hand inside his shirt. "On the loose in the big town, meeting interesting people, seeing the sights . . ."

"A tour of the local dungeons isn't my idea of high living," Lafayette objected. "We can't stay here under this bush; it'll be dawn soon. Our best bet is to try to make it back down to the wharf and sneak aboard our boat, if it's still there."

"You mean you want to leave Port Miasma already? But we ain't even been through the wax museum yet!"

"A regrettable omission; but in view of the habit of the local cops to hang first and look at ID's later, I think I'll have to try to survive without it."

"Well—I guess you got a point there, Lafe. But I heard they got a statue o' Pavingale slaying the gore-worm that's so lifelike you could swear you heard the blood drip."

"It's tempting," O'Leary conceded, "but not quite as tempting as staying alive."

"Hulk ain't going to be glad to see us back," Swinehild predicted.

"You don't have to go," Lafayette said. "You seem to manage quite well here. I'm the one they want to hang on sight. Anyway, I have no intention of going back. What's on the other side of the lake?"

"Nothing much. Wastelands, the Chantspel Mountains, a bunch o' wild men, the Endless Forest, monsters. And the Glass Tree. You know."

"How about cities?"

"They say the Erl-king's got some kind o' layout under the mountains. Why?"

"I won't find the kind of help I need in an underground burrow," Lafayette said doubtfully. "Central wouldn't bother posting a representative anywhere but in a large population center."

"Then I guess you're stuck, Lafe. Port Miasma's the only town in this part o' Melange, as far as I know."

"That's ridiculous," Lafayette scoffed. "There has to be more than one city."

"Why?"

"Well—now that you mention it, I guess there doesn't." He sighed. "And I suppose that means I have to stay and make another try to see the duke. What I need is a disguise: different clothes, a false beard, maybe an eye patch . . ."

"Too bad I didn't pick up a soldier's uniform for you while I had the chance," Swinehild said. "There it was, laying right there on the chair . . ."

"All I need is something to get me through the gate. Once I gained the duke's ear and explained how vital it is I get back to Artesia, my troubles would be over."

"Better take it slow, Lafe. I hear Rodolpho's kind of careful who gets near him these days, ever since some intruder hit him over the head with a chair while he was sitting in it."

"I'll deal with that problem when I get to it," O'Leary said. "But this is all just a lot of air castles. Without a disguise, it's hopeless." He pared another slice from the sausage, chewed at it morosely.

"Don't be downhearted, Lafe," Swinehild cajoled. "Who knows what might turn up? Heck, you might find just what you need hanging on a bush; you never know."

"I wish it was that easy. It used to be that easy. All I had to do was focus the psychic energies and arrange matters as I pleased. Of course, there were limitations. I could only change things that hadn't happened yet, things I hadn't seen—like what was around the next corner."

"Sounds like a swell trick, Lafe," Swinehild said dreamily, joining in the mood. "You could conjure up jewels and black-satin pillers with MOTHER on 'em and Gorp knows what-all."

"I'd settle for a putty nose complete with spectacles, buck teeth, and a toothbrush moustache," Lafayette said. "And maybe a bushy red wig—and a monk's outfit, with a pillow for padding. It would just be lying there under the bushes where somebody lost it, and—" He broke off, his eyes wide open.

"Did you feel that?"

"Uh-uh. Do it again."

"Wasn't there a . . . a sort of . . . thump? As if the world went over a bump in the road?"

"Naw. Now, you was just saying, about the

three wishes and all: I wish I had a pair o' them black-lace step-ins with a little pink ribbon—"

"Swinehild—shhh!" Lafayette interrupted abruptly. He cocked his head, listening. There was a muffled giggle from nearby, accompanied by threshings and puffings as of a friendly wrestling match.

"Wait here." Lafayette crept under the encircling boughs, skirted a stand of dwarf cedar. The sounds were coming from the deep shadows ahead. A dry twig snapped sharply under his hand.

"Hark, Pudelia—what's that?" a jowly voice whispered. The bushes trembled and a pouch-eyed face with a fringe of mouse-colored hair poked forth. For an instant the bulging blue eyes stared directly into O'Leary's paralyzed gaze. Then, with a muffled gobbling sound, it disappeared.

"Your husband!" the voice strangled. "Every man for himself!" There was a squeal, followed by the sound of rapid departures. Lafayette let out a long breath and turned away.

Something caught his eye, draped on the bush. It was a capacious gray robe of coarse wool, well matted with leaves on the underside. Beside it lay a black-satin cushion, lettered INCHON in pink and yellow.

"Great heavens," Lafayette breathed. "Do you suppose . . . ?" He scouted farther, encountered what felt like a small, furry animal. He held it up to the moonlight.

"A . . . a red wig!"

"Lafe—what's going on?" Swinehild whispered from behind him. "Where'd you get that?"

"It was—just lying here."

"And a monk's robe—and my piller!" Swinehild caught up the latter and hugged it. "Lafe—you seen all this stuff before! You was funning me about wishing for it!"

"There ought to be one more item," Lafayette said, scanning the ground. "Ah!" He plucked a false nose with attached spectacles, teeth, and moustache from under the bush.

"And my fancy underdrawers just like I always wanted!" Swinehild yelped in delight, catching a wispy garment. "Lafe, you old tease!" She flung her arms around his neck and kissed him warmly.

"Oh boy," Lafayette said, disengaging himself from her embrace. "I've got my old stuff back. I don't know why, or how, but—" He closed his yes. "Right behind that tree," he murmured. "A Harley-Davidson, fire-engine-red." He paused expectantly, opened one eye, then walked over and looked behind the tree.

"That's funny." He tried again:

"Behind the bench: a Mauser seven-six-five automatic in a black-leather holster, with a spare clip—loaded." He hurried over and rooted unsuccessfully among the leaves.

"I don't get it—first it works and then it doesn't!"

"Aw, never mind, Lafe, it was a good joke, but now, like you said, we got to shake a leg. Lucky for you that local sport tricked hisself out in a friar's costume to meet his doxy. That get-up's better'n a soldier suit."

"Could it have been just coincidence?" O'Leary

muttered as he tucked the pillow inside his belt, pulled on the robe, donned the wig and the nose. Swinehild snickered.

"How do I look?" He rotated before her.

"You look like one o' them strolling minstrels—the Spots Brothers, the smart one— Grumpo."

"Well, it will have to do."

"Sure; it's swell. Listen, Lafe: forget about seeing the duke. You can make like a strolling minstrel yourself. We'll find us a snug garret someplace and fix it up with curtains on the windows and a pot o' pinks, and—"

"Don't talk nonsense, Swinehild," Lafayette reproved her. "Duke Rodolpho's my only hope of getting out of this miserable place."

Swinehild caught at his hand. "Lafe—don't go back to the palace. If they catch you again, this time it'll be zzzt! for sure. Can't you just settle down here and be happy?"

"Happy? You think I enjoy being hit on the head and thrown in jail and hiding in the bushes?"

"I'll . . . I'll hide with you, Lafe."

"There, there, Swinehild, you're a nice girl and I appreciate all your help, but it's out of the question. I have a wife waiting for me, remember?"

"Yeah—but she's there—and I'm here."

He patted her hand. "Swinehild, you run along and pursue your career. I'm sure you're going to be a great success in the big city. As for me, I have more serious business to attend to—alone. Goodbye and good luck."

"D-don't you want to take the lunch?" She offered the bottle and what was left of the sausage.

"In case you wind up back in the pokey?"

"Thanks—you keep it. I don't intend to eat again until I'm dining in style. . . ."

There was a clip-clop of hooves on the street beyond the hedge. Lafayette ducked to the nearest gap and peered through. A party of mounted cuirassiers in lemon-colored coats and plumed helmets was cantering toward him, followed by a matched pair of gleaming black horses with silver-mounted harness drawing a gilt-and-pink coach.

At the open window of the vehicle, Lafayette glimpsed a gloved feminine hand, a sleeve of pale-blue velvet. A face leaned forward in profile, then turned toward him. . . .

"Daphne!" he yelled. The coachman flicked his whip out over the horses; the coach rattled past, gaining speed. Lafayette burst through the hedge and dashed after it, raced alongside. The passenger stared down at him with a wide-eyed look of astonishment.

"Daphne!" O'Leary gasped, grabbing for the door handle. "It is you! Stop! Wait!"

There was a roar from the nearest of the escort; hooves clashed and thundered. A trooper galloped up beside him; Lafayette saw a saber descending in time to duck, trip over a loose cobblestone, and skid two yards on his jaw. He pried his face from the street and saw the coach bowling away across the plaza before his view was cut off by the legs of the prancing horses that had surrounded him. He looked up into the fiercely mustachioed face of the captain of the escort.

"Throw this miserable bum in the dungeons!"

he bellowed. "Truss him in chains! Stretch him on the rack! But don't spoil him! The Lady Andragorre will doubtless want to witness his death throes personally!"

"Daphne," Lafayette mumbled brokenly as a trooper prodded him to his feet with a lance. "And she didn't even look back. . . ."

Five

Lafayette's new cell was somewhat less luxurious than the first he had occupied, featuring a damp floor the size of a card table and a set of leg irons which had been riveted to his ankles, not without occasioning a few bruises. Beyond the bars, a big-armed man in ominous black leathers whistled with more cheer than tune, poking up a merry blaze on a small grate beside which hung an array of curiously shaped tongs, pincers and oversized nutcrackers. To the right of the fireplace was a metal rack resembling an upended bedstead, but for a number of threaded rods running its full length, with crank handles at the ends. Balancing the composition on the left was an open, upended sarcophagus studded with rusted three-inch spikes.

"Listen to me," Lafayette was saying for the ninth time. "If you'll just a get a message to the duke for me, this whole silly misunderstanding will be cleared up!"

"Have a heart, pal." The technician gave O'Leary a weary smile. "For you, this is all new; but I been through it a thousand times. Your best bet is to just relax and keep your mind on something else. Flowers, now. Flowers is nice. Just think about 'em poking up their purty little heads on a spring A.M., all bedewed wit' dew and all. You won't hardly notice what's happening."

"You have more confidence in my powers of contemplation than I do," Lafayette said. "Anyway, my case is different. I'm innocent, just an inoffensive tourist; all I want is a chance to explain matters to his Grace the duke, after which I'll put in a good word for you, and—"

"Tch. You're wasting your wind, fella. You goofed when you didn't ditch your mad-monk suit before you pulled the caper. Half the ducal guard's been combing the town for a week to apprehend that blackguard, which he's pulled ten jobs right under their noses. And you musta been consumed wit' unholy lusts or something to jump her ladyship's carriage right in front of the gate, not that I blame you. She's a looker, all right, all right."

"Is that, er, all they have on me?"

"Jeez, kid, ain't that enough? The duke hisself's got a eye on her Ladyship. He don't take kindly to mugs which they make a pass at her."

"I mean, there isn't any old charge left over from yesterday or anything silly like that? Anything they'd want to, say, cut my head off at dawn for?"

"A beheading rap? Naw, this is nothing like that, just the standard workout wit' the irons and then a nice clean garroting. There *was* a axing slated for dawn, but I heard the guy turned out to be a wizard: he turned into a bat and flew up the chimbley."

"How clever of him. I wish I knew his secret."

Lafayette squeezed his yes shut.

"I'm back in Artesia, out in the desert," he whispered urgently. "It's a nice night, and the stars are shining, and all I have to do is walk about twenty miles through loose sand and I'll be back at the palace and—"

"Hey, nix on the spells," the executioner broke in reproachfully. "You got enough on your plate wit'out a necromancy charge."

"It's no use, anyway," O'Leary groaned. "I thought I had it back, but I guess I was just kidding myself. I'm stuck here—unless I can talk to the duke," he finished on a note of desperation. "Won't you at least try? If I'm telling the truth, it could mean a nice promotion for you."

"I don't need no promotion, chum. I'm already at the top o' my profession; I'm happy wit' my work."

"You enjoy being a torturer?"

"That ain't a term us P.P.S.'s like, mister," the man said in a hurt tone. "What we are, we're Physical-Persuasion Specialists. You don't want to get us mixed up wit' these unlicensed quacks, which they're lousing up the good name of the profession."

"You mean it takes special training to raise a blister with a hot iron?"

"There's more to it than that. You take like the present assignment: I got strict instructions to keep you in what we call an undergraduate status until her Ladyship gets back. And since she figures to be gone a couple weeks, you can see I got a delicate fortnight ahead. Not any slob could do it."

"Say, I have a suggestion," Lafayette offered

brightly. "Why not just kind of forget I'm here until maybe just before the deadline? Then you can paint on a few stripes with Mercurochrome and fake up some wax welts, and—"

"Hold it right there," the P.P.S. cut in sternly. "I'm gonna pretend like I never heard that. Why, if I pulled a stunt like that, I'd be drummed outa the guild."

"Tell you what," O'Leary said. "If you promose not to tell, I won't either."

"Cheese—it's a temptation—but no." The P.P.S. poked at the coals, rotating the iron he was holding to ensure an even cherry-red heat. "I got tradition to think of. The honor of the calling, all that stuff. I mean, it's thoughtful of you, bub, but I couldn't do it." He lifted the glowing poker and studied the color critically, licked a finger and touched it lightly, eliciting a sharp hiss.

"O.K., I guess we're ready. If you don't mind just stripping to the waist, we can get started."

"Oh, no hurry," Lafayette protested, retreating to the back wall of the cell, his hands searching frantically over the rough masonry. *Just one loose stone*, he pleaded silently. *One little old secret tunnel. . . .*

"Candidly, I'm already behind," the P.P.S. said. "What say we warm up on a little light epidermal work, and then move into the pressure centers before we break for midnight snack? Hey, I forgot to ask: you want a box lunch? A buck-fifty, but I hear they got chicken salad tonight and a jelly roll."

"No thanks, I'm on a food-free diet for the duration. Did I mention I'm under a physician's care?

No sudden shocks, particularly electrical ones, and—"

"If it was me, I'd throw the chow in free, you know, American plan. But—"

"What do you know about America?" Lafayette blurted.

"Everybody knows Luigi America, the big noodle and egg man. Too bad the duke's too tight to go along wit' the meal-ticket scheme—"

"I heard that, Groanwelt," a resonant baritone voice rang out. A tall, well-muscled but slightly paunchy man with smooth gray hair and rimless glasses had stepped through a door in the far wall. He wore tight-fitting yellow trousers, red-leather shoes with curled-up toes, a ruffled shirt, a short cloak trimmed with ermine. Jewels sparkled on his fingers. Lafayette looked at him, speechless.

"Oh, hi, your Grace," the torturer said casually. "Well, you know I never say anything behind your back I w'unt say to your face."

"One day you'll go too far," the newcomer snapped. "Leave us now. I'll have a word with the prisoner."

"Hey, no fair, your Grace; I just got my number-four iron up to operating temperature!"

"Need I point out that I would find it somewhat difficult to carry on a lucid conversation with your client amidst an odor of roasting callus?"

"Yeah—I guess you got a point." Groanwelt shoved the iron back into the coals and cast a regretful look at O'Leary. "Sorry, chum. But you see how it is."

The gray-haired man was studying O'Leary with narrowed eyes. As soon as the door had closed behind the P.P.S., he stepped close to the bars.

"So it *is* you," he said and broke off, frowning. "What's the matter with you?" he demanded sharply. "You look as if you'd seen a ghost."

"N-N-Nicodaeus?" O'Leary whispered.

"If that's supposed to be some kind of password, I don't recognize it," Duke Rodolpho barked.

"You're . . . not Nicodaeus? You aren't a subinspector of continua? You can't make a fast phone call and have me whisked back to Artesia?"

The duke glared at O'Leary.

"Enough of these obfuscations, Lancelot. First you burst into my audience chamber spouting nonsense; then you escape from my maximumsecurity dungeon under the very eyes of my alert guard staff. Next, you openly appear in a waterfront dive, fairly begging to be brought in again—whereupon you once more fly the coop—only to invite arrest a third time by accosting a certain great lady in full view of her guard. Very well, I may be a bit obtuse, but I think I get the message: you have something to sell."

"Oh?" Lafayette squealed. "That is, oh. So you finally caught on."

"And?" Rodolpho glared.

"And, uh . . . what?" O'Leary inquired brightly. The duke frowned.

"So you intend to keep me on tenterhooks, do you? Well, it won't wash, fellow! Disappear again, go ahead, amuse yourself! But don't expect me to come crawling to you begging for information regarding the Lady Andragorre . . ." He finished on a semi-interrogative note, almost a pleading look in his eyes.

"Lady Andragorre?" Lafayette mumbled. "Me, tell you . . . ?"

"Very well," the duke sighed. "I can see I've handled you wrongly from the beginning, Lancelot. All right, I acknowledge my mistake. But you can hardly blame me, considering the affair of the poached egg and the incident of the bladder of ink! Still, I'm ready to make amends. I'll even apologize, though it goes against the grain. Now will you consent to sit down with me and discuss this matter in gentlemanly fashion?"

"Well, ah, of course I want to be reasonable," Lafayette ad-libbed desperately. "But a torture chamber is hardly the proper surroundings for a heart-to-heart."

The duke grunted. He turned and yelled for Groanwelt.

"See that this nobleman is released, washed, fed, garbed as befits his station, and brought to my apartment in half an hour," he commanded. He gave O'Leary a sharp look. "No disappearing until then, Lancelot," he said gruffly, and stalked from the room.

"Well, that's the breaks," Groanwelt said philosophically as he unlocked the door. "Looks like we don't get together on a professional basis tonight after all. But it was swell meeting you anyway, kid. Maybe some other time."

"I wouldn't doubt it," Lafayette aid. "Say, Groanwelt, what do you know about this, er, Lady Andragorre?"

"Nothing special. Just that she's the richest, most beautiful dame in Melange, is all, which the duke is carrying a torch the size of the Chicago fire for her."

"You know about the Chicago fire?"

"Sure. A beer joint. Burned down last week. Why?"

"Never mind. You were saying?"

"Too bad fer his Grace, he'll never get to first base wit' her Ladyship."

"Why not?"

Groanwelt leered and lowered his voice. "On account of there's another guy, natch. It's the talk of the locker rooms."

"Another guy?" Lafayette felt his heart lurch violently under his sternum.

Groanwelt dug an elbow into Lafayette's ribs. "Duke Rodolpho don't know it, but he's playing second fiddle to a rogue name of Lorenzo the Lanky—or is it Lancelot the Lucky?"

"Lorenzo the Lanky?" Lafayette croaked as Groanwelt struck off his gyves.

"As a matter of fact," the P.P.S. said in the tone of one who imparts a confidence, "right now milady is officially on her way to visit her old-maid aunt and twelve cats. But between you and me, the word is she's headed for a hunting lodge in the Chantspels for a trial honeymoon wit' the lucky geezer."

"T-trial honeymoon?"

"Yep. Now, let's go turn you over to the chamberlain, which he'll doll you up in shape for yer audience wit' his Grace."

Duke Rodolpho was sitting in a big soft-leather wing chair when Lafayette was shown in, clean and fragrant and dressed in a fresh outfit of spangled silk which almost fit.

"Sit down, Lancelot," the duke ordered with an air of forced cordiality. "Drink? Cigar?" He waved a hand, which took in a deep easy chair, a low table with a decanter and glasses, and a humidor.

"Thanks." Lafayette flopped gratefully, then yawned earcrackingly. "Sorry. I'm up past my bedtime. By the way, my name's Lafayette."

"You dined adequately?"

"As adequately as you can while six handmaidens are scrubbing your back, putting Band-Aids on your hurties, and massaging your bruises. Not that I didn't appreciate the attention."

"Excellent. Now let's not beat around the cactus bed, Lancelot. Just what is your, ah, connection with the Lady Andragorre?" The duke nipped at a hangnail, eyeing Lafayette sharply.

"My connection with the Lady Andragorre," Lafayette temporized. "Well, ah, as to that—the fact is, I'm her husband."

The duke's face went rigid. "Her husband?" His voice cracked like a snapped neck.

"Her estranged husband," O'Leary amended hurriedly. "As a matter of fact, we're practically strangers."

"I had never heard that milady had been married," Rodolpho said in a dangerous tone. He reached to pour himself a stiff jolt of brandy, tossed it back in a gulp. "Much less divorced."

"She's a charming girl," Lafayette hurried on. "Full of fun, lighthearted—"

"You may skip over the intimate revelations," Rodolpho snapped. He chewed his lip. "Perhaps this explains Captain Ritzpaugh's report that you attempted to speak to her in the street and were repulsed with a riding crop."

"He's a"—Lafayette started—"a very perceptive fellow," he finished.

"One wonders what offense you committed to earn such detestation from so high-bred a lady."

"Well, I think It all started with crackers in bed," O'Leary began, then noted the black frown spreading over the ducal features. "Crackers is her cat," he improvised hastily. "She insisted on sleeping with her. And since I'm allergic to cats—well, you can see it wasn't much of a marriage."

"You mean—you never—you didn't—"

"Right." Lafayette used his lace cuff to wipe the dew from his brow and poured out a revivifying draft for himself.

"That's well for you, Lancelot," Rodolpho said in steely tones. "Otherwise I'd be forced to order your instant execution."

"Lafayette. And let's not start that again," O'Leary said, shuddering with the strong spirits. "You had me dusted off and brought up here for a reason. Let's get on with it."

The duke started to drum his fingers on the table, halted them abruptly. "I have conceived an infatuation for the lady," he said brusquely. "Accordingly, I invited her to spend a weekend with me at my winter palace. Instead of accepting the honor with alacrity, she pleaded a previous appointment with an aged relative."

"And?"

"Perhaps I'm overly sensitive, but I imagined

just the faintest hint of coolness in her manner."
The duke poured himself another peg.

"Maybe you're not her type," Lafayette
suggested, following suit.

"Not her type? What do you mean?"

"Well, for one thing, you're old enough to be
her father," O'Leary pointed out.

"That's unimportant!"

"Maybe not to her. Also, if you don't mind my
saying so, you don't have what I'd call exactly a
jolly manner about you. Daph—I mean the Lady
Andragorre's a fun-loving kid—"

"A jolly manner? How can I be jolly, burdened
as I am with affairs of state, indigestion, insomnia,
and an unfavorable balance of payments?" The
duke grabbed the bottle and poured, belatedly
filled Lafayette's glass as he held it out.

"That's just it, your Grace. All work and no play
makes Rodolpho a dull fellow."

"All work and no—by gad, sir, well put!" They
clicked glasses and swallowed. The duke licked
his lips thoughtfully. "I see it now. What an idiot
I've been! Why didn't I just go to her openly,
suggest a gay afternoon of mummy-viewing at the
local museum, or possibly a wild, abandoned
evening of canasta? But no: all I ever offered her
was state dinners and tickets to the visitors' box at
the weekly meetings of the Fiduciary Council."

"That's the idea, Rodolpho." Lafayette poured
this time. "You might even go all out and propose
a walk in the park, or a swim at the beach, or even
a picnic on the lawn. There's nothing like a few
ants in the potato salad to break down the barriers.
Skål."

"Of course, my boy! Why didn't it occur to me sooner?" Rodolpho splashed brandy on the table in the process of filling the glasses. "I've been a fool. A stodgy, imperceptive idiot."

"Don't blame yourself, Rudy," Lafayette said, raising his glass. "After all, you had the duchy to run."

"True. But now everything's going to be different, thanks to you, lad. I'll ply her with my favorite viands, treat her to the music I like best, overwhelm her with my preference in wines, literature, and perfume, shower her with the kind of clothes I think she ought to wear—"

"Slow down, Rudy." Lafayette wagged an admonitory finger. "How about giving some thought to the little lady's tastes?"

"Eh? How could she object to chopped chicken livers washed down with Pepsi and Mogen David while a steel band plays variations on the theme from the 'Dead March from *Saul*'?"

"While wearing a Mother Hubbard reeking of *Nuit de Gimbel's*? Hard to say, Rudy. But women are strange little beasts. You can never tell what they're thinking. Remind me to tell you about the princess I was once engaged to—"

"I'll do it now—tonight!" Rodolpho exclaimed, and banged his fist on the tray. "I'll—but hang it all, I can't! She's out of town, won't be back for a fortnight."

"She was a swell-looking girl, too," Lafayette said. "But the minute my back was turned—"

"But, blast it, what's the good in being duke if I can't have my own way?" Rodolpho looked triumphantly at Lafayette. "I'll have her brought back. A fast troop of cavalry can overtake her entourage in a couple of hours, which will just give me time to chill the Pepsi and—"

"Ah, ah, Rudy," O'Leary objected. "Cajolery, not force, remember?"

"But force is so much quicker."

"Do you want a whipped slave, sullenly doing your bidding—or a willing *petite amie*, charmed into your web by your munificence and consideration?"

"Hmmm. The slave approach is probably the more practical, now you mention it."

"Nonsense, Rudy. You want this lovely little piece of ripe fruit to drop into your hand, right? So instead of having a bunch of sweaty soldiers on lathered horses haul her back to you kicking and scratching, you need an envoy who can convey your wishes with the delicacy appropriate to so tender a mission." Lafayette hiccuped and upended the bottle over his glass.

"Egad, son, you're right, as usual." Rodolpho frowned thoughtfully. "But who among this collection of cretins and dullards who surround me can I entrust with the task?"

"You need a man of proven ability, ingenuity, and courage. Somebody who won't sell the horse and auction off the autograph on your letter as soon as he's out of sight of the castle walls. A gentleman-adventurer, resourceful, intrepid, dedicated—"

"What letter?"

"The one you're going to write, to tell her how you've been worshipping her from afar," O'Leary said. He shook the empty bottle and tossed it over his shoulder.

"A capital notion!" Rodolpho exclaimed, and

banged the tray again, upsetting the glasses. "But—but what will I say?" He gnawed the outer corner of his left ring finger. "Candidly, my boy—"

"Just call me Lafayette, Rudy."

"I thought it was Lancelot," the duke said. "But never mind. Candidly, as I say, I've never been much of a one for writing flowery language—"

"Where did you get that idea?"

"Why, you suggested it."

"I didn't mean that, I meant the idea my name was Lancelot."

"Lancelot—what about it?" Rodolpho looked blank, then brightened. "Of course!" he exclaimed, expelling a scrap of fingernail from the tip of his tongue. "Just the man for it! You're ingenious, intrepid, and have a sound head on your shoulders. Do you drink?" he asked in an abruptly challenging tone.

"Not when the bottle's empty."

"Excellent. Never trust a man who can't handle his liquor. By the way, the bottle's empty." Rodolpho rose and made his way across the room, bucking powerful crosswinds, opened a cabinet, extracted a fresh fifth, and navigated back to his chair.

"Now, as I was saying: go to this person, Lancelot, pour out your heart to her, explain that it's woman's highest duty to fetch and carry for her lord and master, and that while you can offer her only the miserable life of a serf, she can draw comfort from the fact that she won't live forever."

"That's certainly a persuasive approach," Lafayette said, wrestling the cork from the bottle. "But I had a funny idea it was you that wanted the girl." He frowned, straining to focus his eyes. "Or am I confused?"

"By gad, Lancelot, you're right. I am the one who wants her." The duke shot Lafayette a hostile look. "I must say it's cheeky of you to attempt to try to come between us. The minx is mad about me, but being a trifle shy, I'm thinking of sending a trusted emissary to drag her back billing and cooing. I mean coax her back kicking and screaming."

"A capital idea," Lafayette agreed, pouring a stream of brandy between the two glasses. "Who do you have in mind?"

"Well—how about Groanwelt?"

"Positively not. No diplomatesse, if you know what I mean."

"Lancelot! I've a splendid notion. Why don't you go?"

"Not a chance, Rudy," Lafayette said. "You're just trying to distract me from my real mission."

"What mission?"

"To get you to send me after the Lady Andragorre."

"Out of the question! You presume too far!" Rodolpho grabbed the bottle and splashed brandy across the glasses.

"What about a compromise?" Lafayette suggested with a crafty look.

"What do you have in mind?"

"I'll deliver your letter to the lady—in return for which you appoint me your messenger. Or is it vice versa?"

"That seems fair. Now, when you catch up with her, you're to tell her of my deep attachment, explain in detail my many sterling qualities, and

in short, overwhelm her with the picture of the
good fortune which has befallen her."

"Anything else?"

"Absolutely not!" Rodolpho looked sternly at a
point to the right of O'Leary's ear. "I'll handle the
courtship from that point on."

"All right, Rudy—I'll undertake this assignment. You did right to come to me."

"I knew I could count on you," the duke said
brokenly. He rose and handed over a massive ring.
"This signet will secure the cooperation of my
staff." He held out his hand. "I'll never forget this,
old man. You've given me new hope."

"Think nothing of it, Rudy. Now you'd better
run along. I'm pooped. Got a big day tomorrow."

"What's tomorrow?"

"Tuesday."

"Of course. And speaking of tomorrow, I may
have a surprise in store for you. Don't tell anybody, but a little birdie told me a certain lady may
be calling."

"Rudy! You lucky dog! Congratulations!"

"But don't bruit it about. Bad luck, you know.
Well, I really must be going. Jolly evening and all
that."

"Don't rush off. We were just getting started."
Lafayette held up the half-full bottle and blinked
at it. "Hardly touched it," he pointed out.

"I never go near alcohol," the duke said stiffly.
"Rots the brain, I'm told. Good night, Lancelot."
He tottered uncertainly to the door and out.

For a moment after Rodolpho had left, Lafayette
stood swaying in the center of the room, which
seemed to have developed a fairly rapid rotation.
He made his way across to the bathroom, sluiced

cold water over his face, toweled his head vigorously. In the duke's closet he found a capacious fleece-lined riding cloak. He helped himself to a handful of cigars from the ducal humidor, tucked a pair of riding gloves into his pocket, and let himself out into the corridor.

The head groom woke, knuckling his eyes as O'Leary demanded the best horse in the ducal stables. Five minutes later, reeling slightly in the saddle, O'Leary showed the ring at the gate. The guards grumbled but opened up for him. He cantered down through the dark street to the waterfront, used the ring to requisition the ducal barge, ignoring the bargeman's muttered complaints. An hour later, after a chilly crossing, with the first twinges of a hangover stabbing at his temples, he stepped ashore on the west bank of the lake. A narrow, rutted track led up from the jetty into the forest.

"Is that the way the Lady Andragorre's party went?" he inquired of the shivering boatman. "Up that cowpath?"

"Yeah—if you can call it a party, on a night like this." The man blew on his hands. "Snow'll fly before dawn, mark my words, squire."

"Swell," Lafayette said into his turned-up collar. "That's all I need to make this a perfect night." He set spurs to the horse and moved off into the blackness among the trees.

Six

For the next two hours Lafayette followed the winding trail steadily up among the giant trees, past looming boulders and small, rushing streams which spilled down over moss-grown rock formations. The marks of wheels were visible intermittently in the dust, overlain by the hoofprints of the escort. His head throbbed. The cold wind slashed at him through his cloak. As far as evidence to the contrary indicated, he was making no progress whatever.

"It's probably a wild-duck chase," he mumbled to himself. "I've done nothing but blunder from the beginning. First, by not insisting that that chap Pratwick put me through to his supervisor. But I was so rattled I hardly knew where I was—and still don't, for that matter. Melange. Who's ever heard of it? And Port Miasma: a pesthole if there ever was one. . . ."

And he'd goofed again by getting mixed up with Swinehild. Strange, her looking so much like Adoranne. Poor kid, she'd been badly enough off before he arrived. He'd only been here twelve hours or so, and already he'd broken up a home.

And then being idiot enough to fall afoul of the cops; and then that supreme triumph of the blunderer's art, leaping at Daphne's—that is, Lady Andragorre's—carriage. He should have known she wouldn't know him; nobody around this insane place was what they seemed. And then all that persiflage with the duke. . . .

"Why did I sit around half the night trying to drink Rodolpho under the table, while Lady Andragorre rode off into the distance?" he groaned. "In fact, why am I here at all? If I do find her, I'll probably end up getting that riding crop Rudy mentioned across the chops for my pains. But what else could I do? If she isn't Daphne, she's her twin. I can't very well let her fall into the clutches of this Lorenzo the Lanky character. Or is it Lancelot the Lucky?"

He shifted in the saddle. The cold had numbed his toes and ears and fingers. Was he gaining on the quarry or falling behind? The tracks looked no fresher than they had when he started.

He flapped the reins, urging his mount into a canter. The beast clattered up the trail, snorting steam, while Lafayette crouched low on its neck, ducking under the pine boughs that brushed his back. He rounded a turn, caught a glimpse of something bulky blocking the path ahead. He reined in sharply.

"Oh-oh," he said, feeling a sudden dryness in his mouth. "Dirty work's afoot. . . ."

It was Lady Andragorre's pink coach, standing silent in the center of the track, one door swinging in the gusty wind. Lafayette dismounted, wincing at the ache behind his eyes, walked up beside it, glanced into the rose-velvet interior. A lacy handkerchief lay on the pink lamb's-wool rug. He picked it up, sniffed it.

"Moonlight Rose, Daphne's favorite," he groaned.

The traces, he found, had been cut. There was no sign of the four splendid blacks, or of the escort, other than a confused spoor leading on up the trail.

"Funny there are no bodies lying around," Lafayette muttered. "But I suppose the cowardly louses surrendered without a struggle." As he turned back toward his horse, there was a crackling in the underbrush beside the trail. Lafayette grabbed for the ornamental sword with which the duke's servants had provided him.

"Not another move, or I'll punch a hole through your treacherous weasand," a voice rasped behind him. He spun, looked into a scowling, mustachioed face, and the tip of a bared blade inches from his throat. Other men were emerging from concealment, swords in hand. Lafayette was just realizing that they wore the yellow livery of the Lady Andragorre's household, when rough hands seized his arms from behind.

"Came back to gloat, did you? Or was it loot you had in mind?" The captain poked the sword at Lafayette's midriff. "Where is she, miserable wretch!"

"I w-was just going to ask you that question!"

"Speak—or I may not be able to restrain my lads from ripping your carcass limb from limb!"

"You were escorting her." Lafayette found his voice. "Why ask me where she is? What did you do, run off and leave her?"

"Ah-hah, so that's the game, is it? Next I sup-

pose you'll demand ransom for her return!"
Lafayette yipped as the point pinked him again.
"I'll ransom you, you sneaking snake in the underbrush! Talk! What have you done with the
finest little mistress a squadron of cavalry ever
had!"

"I'm on official business," Lafayette panted.
"Take a look at the signet on my left hand."

Hard hands fumbled with the massive ring.

"It won't come off," a corporal reported. "Want
me to cut it off?"

"You think to bribe us with this bauble?" the
captain barked.

"Of course not! It belongs to Duke Rodolpho!
But the finger's mine. Do you mind leaving it
where it is?"

"Boy, what a nerve, to swipe the duke's ring
and then have the gall to brag about it," the troop
sergeant growled.

"I didn't steal it, he gave it to me!"

"Let's run the bum through, Cap'n," a trooper
spoke up. "I got no use for guys which they're
such lousy liars. Everybody knows his Grace is
tighter than a thumbscrew."

"Can't you get it through your thick heads I'm
not a kidnapper? I'm on an important mission,
and—"

"What mission?"

"To catch up with the Lady Andragorre, and
bring her back—"

"So you admit it!"

"But I had no intention of doing it," O'Leary
amplified, struggling to force his throbbing head
to function effectively. "I intended to head in the
opposite direction, and—"

"And lingered a bit too long about the scene of your dastardly abduction!" the captain snarled. "Very well, fetch rope, men! His dangling corpse will serve as a warning to others!"

"Wait!" Lafayette shouted. "I give up, you're too smart for me. I'll . . . I'll talk!"

"Very well." The captain jabbed him. "Talk!"

"Well, let's see . . . where shall I begin," O'Leary stalled.

"Start with when Lou had to step into the bushes," the sergeant suggested.

"Yes, well, as soon as Lou stepped into the bushes, I, ah . . ."

"You hit him over the head, right?" a trooper contributed.

"Right. And then, er . . ."

"Then when we held up and sent a couple guys back to see what was taking Lou so long, you bopped them on the knob too, right?"

"That's it—"

"And then, while the rest of us was beating the brush for the boys which they hadn't come back, you nips in and whisks her Ladyship away from under the nose of Les, which he was holding the nags, right?"

"Who's telling this, you or me?" O'Leary inquired tartly.

"So where is she now?"

"How do I know? I was busy hitting Lou over the head and whisking around under Les's nose, remember?"

"How come you know the boys' names? You been casing this job a long time, hey?"

"Never mind that, Quackwell," the captain barked. "We're wasting time. The lady's whereabouts, you, or I'll stretch your neck i' the instant!''

"She's—she's at the hunting lodge of Lorenzo the Lanky!"

"Lorenzo the Lanky? And where might this lodge be found?"

"It's, er, right up this trail a few miles."

"Liar," the officer barked. "This road leads nowhere save to the château of milady's Aunt Prussic!"

"Are you sure of that?" Lafayette shot back.

"Certainly. Milady herself so informed me."

"Well, your intelligence apparatus needs overhauling," Lafayette snapped. "It's the talk of the locker rooms that Lorenzo the Lanky lives up this way. Or maybe Lochinvar—or is it Lothario? . . ."

"I fail to grasp the import of your slimy innuendos, varlet," the captain said in a deadly tone. "Wouldst have me believe that milady deliberately misled me? That she in fact had arranged some clandestine rendezvous with this Lorenzo, here in the depths of the Chantspels?"

"It wouldn't be very clandestine, with a dozen pony soldiers hanging around," O'Leary pointed out.

"You mean—you think she ditched us on purpose?" The N.C.O. scowled ferociously.

"Use your heads," Lafayette said. "If I'd taken her, do you think I'd leave her and come nosing back around here, just so you could catch me?"

"Enough of your vile implications, knave!" the

captain barked. "Stand back, men! I'll deal with this blackguard!"

"Hey, hold it, Cap," the sergeant said, tugging at his forelock. "Begging the captain's pardon, but what the guy says makes sense. It was her Ladyship that said we ought to go back and look for Whitey and Fred, right?"

"Yeah, and also, come to think about it, I never heard before about her having no aunt living out in the boondocks," a trooper added.

"Preposterous," the captain said in a tone lacking in conviction. "Her Ladyship would never thus cozen me, her faithful liegeman, in such fashion!"

"I dunno, Cap. Dames. Who knows from dames, what they might do?"

"Mind your tongue!" The captain yanked at his tunic with a decisive gesture. "I'll soil my ears with no more of the knave's preposterous inventions. On with the hanging!"

"Now, don't be hasty, fellows," O'Leary yelled. "I'm telling you the truth! Lady Andragorre is probably just a few miles ahead; we ought to be galloping to overtake her instead of standing around here arguing!"

"He seeks to mislead us!" the captain snapped. "Doubtless milady lies trussed where he left her, mere yards from this spot!"

"He's out of his skull!" Lafayette protested. "He's afraid to go after her! This is just an excuse to muddy the waters and turn back!"

"Enough! Prepare the criminal for execution!"

"Wait!" Lafayette cried as the noose dropped

around his neck. "Can't we settle this like gentle-men?"

A sudden silence fell. The sergeant was looking at the captain, who was frowning blackly at O'Leary.

"You demand the treatment accorded a gentleman? On what grounds?"

"I'm Sir Lafayette O'Leary, a—a charter member of the National Geographic Society!"

"Looks like he's got something, Cap," the sergeant said. "With credentials like them, you can't hardly accord the guy short shrift."

"He's right," Lafayette said hastily. "I'm sure that on sober reflection you can see it wouldn't look at all well if you lynched me."

" 'Tis a parlous waste of time," the captain growled. "But—very well. Remove the rope."

"Well, I'm glad we're all going to be friends," Lafayette said. "Now, I—"

"Out pistols!"

"Wha—what are you going to do with those?" Lafayette inquired as the troopers unlimbered foot-long horse pistols, busied themselves with flint and priming.

"Take up your stance against yon tree, sir knight," the captain barked. "And be quick about it. We haven't got all night!"

"Y-you mean this tree?" Lafayette half-stumbled over gnarly roots. "Why? What . . . ?"

"Ready, men! Aim!"

"Stop!" O'Leary called in a cracking voice. "You can't shoot me!"

"You demanded a gentleman's death, did you not? Aim—"

"But—you're not going to fire from *that*

range?" Lafayette protested. "I thought you fellows were marksmen!"

"We took first place in the police tournament last June," the sergeant stated.

"Why don't I just move back a little farther?" Lafayette suggested. "Give you a chance to show your skill." He backed ten feet, bumped another tree.

"Ready!" the captain called. "Aim—"

"Still too close," Lafayette called, wagging a finger. "Let's make it a real challenge." He hastily scrambled back an additional four yards.

"That's far enough!" the captain bellowed. "Stand and receive your fate, sirrah!" He brandished his saber. "Ready! Aim!" As the officer's lips formed the final word, there was a sudden, shrill yowl from the dense brush behind him. All eyes snapped in the direction from which the nerve-shredding sound had come.

"Night cat!" a man blurted. Without waiting for a glimpse of the creature, Lafayette bounded sideways, dived behind the tree, scrambled to his feet, and pelted full speed into the forest, while shouts rang and guns boomed and lead balls screamed through the underbrush around him.

The moon was out, shining whitely on the split-log front of a small cabin situated in the center of a hollow ringed in by giant trees. Lafayette lay on his stomach under a bramble bush, aching all over from a combination of hangover, fatigue, and contusions. It had been thirty minutes since the last halloo had sounded from the troops beating the brush for him, twenty since he had topped the rim of the bowl and seen the dim-lit windows of the hut below. In that time nothing had stirred there, no sound had broken the stillness. And nothing, Lafayette added, had interfered with the development of a classic case of chilblains. The temperature had dropped steadily as the night wore on; now ice crystals glittered on the leaves. Lafayette blew on his hands and stared at the lighted window of the tiny dwelling below.

"She has to be down there," he assured himself. "Where else could she be, in this wilderness?" Of course, he continued the line of thought, whoever kidnapped her is probably there too, waiting with loaded pistols to see if anyone's following. . . .

"On the other hand, if I stay here I'll freeze," O'Leary countered decisively. He tottered to his feet, beat his stiffening arms across his chest, eliciting a hacking cough, then began to make his way cautiously down the shadowy slope. At a distance he circled the house, pausing at intervals, alert for sounds of approaching horsemen or awakening householders; but the silence remained unbroken. The flowered curtains at the small windows blocked his view of the interior.

Lafayette slipped up close to the narrow back door, flanked by a pile of split wood and a rain barrel; he put an ear against the rough panels.

There was a faint creaking, an even fainter, intermittent popping sound. A low voice was moaning words too faint to distinguish. Lafayette felt a distinct chill creep up his backbone. Early memories of Hansel and Gretel and the witch's cottage rose to vivid clarity.

"Nonsense," he told himself sternly. "There's

no such thing as a witch. There's nobody in there but this Lorenzo operator, and poor Lady Andragorre, probably tied hand and foot, scared to death, hoping against hope that someone will come along and rescue her, poor kid. So why am I standing around waiting? Why don't I kick the door down and drag this Lorenzo out by the scruff of the neck, and . . ."

The popping sound rose to a frantic crescendo and ceased abruptly. There was a soft *whoosh!*, a faint clank of metal. The creaking resumed, accompanied now by a stealthy crunching, as of a meat grinder crushing small bones.

"Maybe he's torturing her, the monster!" Lafayette took three steps back, braced himself, and hurled himself at the door. It flew wide at the impact, and he skidded to the center of a cozy room where a fire glowed on a grate, casting a rosy light on an elderly woman seated in a rocker on a hooked rug, a cat in her lap and a blue china bowl at her elbow.

"Why, Lorenzo, welcome back," she said in tones of mild surprise. She held out the bowl. "Have some popcorn."

Sitting by the fire with a bowl of crisp, lightly buttered and salted kernels on one knee and a cup of thick cocoa on the other, Lafayette attempted to bring his reeling throughts to order. His hostess was stitching away at a quilt she had exhumed from a chest under the window, chattering in a scratchy monotone. He couldn't seem to follow just what it was she was saying—something about a little cuckoo fluttering from flower to flower and settling down in a big soft blossom to snooze. . . .

Lafayette came awake with a start as his chin bumped his chest.

"Why, you're sleepy, poor lad. And no wonder, the hours you've been keeping. Oh, I almost forgot: your friends were here." She gave him a sharp sideways smile.

"Friends?" Lafayette yawned. How long had it been since he had slept? A week? Or only three days . . . or . . . was it possible it was only last night, curled up in the big bed with the silken sheets . . .

". . . said not to bother telling you, they wanted to surprise you. But I thought you'd rather know." Her tone had a sharp edge, penetrating his drowsiness.

Lafayette forced his mind to focus on what the old lady was saying. Her voice seemed vaguely familiar. Had he met her before? Or . . .

"Rather know, ah, what?" He forced his thoughts back to the conversation.

"About them coming back."

"Er, who?"

"The nice gentlemen with the lovely horses."

Suddenly Lafayette was wide awake. "When were they here?"

"Why, you just missed them, Lorenzo—by about thirty minutes." Dim old eyes bored into him through thick glasses. Or were they dim and old? On second look, they were remarkedly sharp. Where, Lafayette wondered, had he seen that gimlet gaze before? . . .

"Ma'am—you've been very kind, but I really must rush. And I think you ought to know: I'm not Lorenzo."

"Not Lorenzo? Whatever do you mean?" She peered over her lenses at him.

"I came here looking for a fellow named Lorenzo, or possibly Lothario or Lancelot. When you welcomed me so nicely, and offered me food and warmth, I, well—I was starving and freezing and I simply took advantage of your kindness. But now I'll be going—"

"Why, I wouldn't hear of it! A body could catch his death on a night like this—"

"I'm not sure you understand," Lafayette protested, sidling toward the door. "I'm a total stranger. I just wandered in here, and—"

"But surely you're the same charming young man who rented the spare bedroom?" The old lady peered nearsightedly at him.

Lafayette shook his head. "Afraid not. I came here looking for the Lady Andragorre—"

"Why, you're a friend of my niece! How delightful! Why didn't you tell me! Now you really must give up this silly idea of going back out in that icy wind. Oh, by the way, ah, where is dear Andi? I had a foolish notion you might be bringing her along?"

"You're Daph—I mean Lady Andragorre's aunt?"

"Why, yes, didn't you know? But you haven't said where she is . . ."

Lafayette was looking around the room. It was clean and comfortable enough, but decidedly on the primitive side. "I got the impression the Lady Andragorre is very well off," he said. "Is this the best she can do for you?"

"Why, foolish boy, I adore living here among the birds and flowers. So quaint and picturesque."

"Who chops the wood?"

"Why, ah, I have a man who comes in on Tuesdays. But you were saying about Lady Andragorre . . . ?"

"I wasn't saying. But I don't know where she is; I came alone. Well, thanks for the goodies—"

"You're not leaving," the old lady said sharply. She smiled. "I won't think of it."

Lafayette pulled on his cloak, went to the door. "I'm afraid I have to decline your hospitality—" He broke off at a sudden sound, turned in time to see the old lady behind him, her had swinging down edge-on in a murderous chop at his temple. He ducked, took the blow on a forearm, yelled at the pain, countered a second vicious swing, aimed a stiff-fingered punch at his hostess's ribs, took a jab to the solar plexus, and fell backward over the rocker.

"Double-crosser!" the old lady yelled. "Selling out to that long-nosed Rodolpho, after all I've promised to do for you! Of all the cast-iron stitch-welded gall, to come waltzing in here pretending you never saw me before!" Lafayette rolled aside as the old lady bounded across the chair, barely fending her off with a kick to the short ribs as he scrambled to his feet.

"Where is she, curse you? Oh, I should have left you tending swine back in that bog I picked you out of—"

Abruptly the old girl halted in mid-swing, cupped an ear. Faintly, O'Leary heard the thud of approaching hooves.

"Blast!" The old woman bounded to the door, snatched a cloak from the peg, whirled it about herself.

"I'll get you for this, Lorenzo!" she keened in a voice that had dropped from a wheezy soprano to a ragged tenor. "Just you wait, my boy! I'll extract a vengeance from you that will make you curse the day you ever saw the Glass Tree!" She yanked the door open and was gone into the night.

Belatedly, O'Leary sprang after her. Ten feet from the door, she stood fiddling with her buttons. As O'Leary leaped, she emitted a loud buzzing hum, bounded into the air, and shot away toward the forest, rapidly gaining altitude, her cloak streaming behind her.

"Hey," Lafayette called weakly. Suddenly he was aware of the rising thunder of hooves. He dashed back inside, across the room, out the back door, and keeping the house between himself and the arriving cavalry, he sprinted for the shelter of the woods.

Dawn came, gray and blustery, hardly lessening the darkness. Lafayette sat in deep gloom under a tree big enough to cut a tunnel through, shivering. His head ached; his stomach had a slow fire in it; his eyeballs felt as if they had been taken out, rolled in corn meal, and Southern-fried. The taste in his mouth resembled pickled onions—spoiled ones. In the branches overhead, a bird squawked mournfully.

"This is it," Lafayette muttered, "the low point of my career. I'm sick, freezing, starving, hungover, and dyspeptic. I've lost my horse, Lady Andragorre's trail—everything. I don't know where I'm going, or what to do when I get there. Also, I'm hallucinating. Flying old ladies, ha! I probably imagined the whole business about the cottage. A dying delirium, maybe I was actually shot by those bumbling incompetents in the yellow coats. Maybe I'm dead!"

He felt himself over, failed to find any bullet holes.

"But this is ridiculous. If I were dead, I wouldn't have a headache." He hitched up his sword belt, tottered a few feet to a small stream, knelt, and sluiced ice water over his face, scrubbed at it with the edge of his cloak, drank a few swallows.

"O.K.," he told himself sternly. "No use standing around talking to myself. This is a time for action.

"Swell," he replied. "What action?

"I could start walking," he suggested. "It's only about twenty miles back to Port Miasma.

"Rodolpho isn't likely to be overjoyed to see me coming back empty-handed," he countered. "But I'll probably have a chance to explain my reasons—to Groanwelt. Anyway, I don't know which direction it is." Lafayette peered upward through the canopy of high foliage. Not even a faint glow against the visible patches of gray sky indicated the position of the sun.

"Besides which, I can't run off and leave the Lady Andragorre to her fate.

"All right, I'm convinced: I press on. Which way is on?"

He turned around three times, with his eyes shut, stopped, and pointed.

"That way."

"You know," O'Leary confided in himself as he started off in the indicated direction, "this talking to myself isn't such a bad idea. It opens up whole new vistas.

"And it certainly cuts down on the shilly-shally factor.

"Of course, it *is* a sign of insanity.

"Poof—what's a little touch of schizophrenia, among all my other ailments?"

He pushed on, limping alternately on the left and right ankles, both of which he had twisted during his several sprints, leaps, and falls of the night before. Gradually the trees thinned; the tangled vines and undergrowth thickened. Patches of bare rock showed through the greenery. As he emerged on a bare, wind-swept slope dotted with stunted, wind-twisted cedars, it began to rain, a needle-sharp spray that stung his eyes, numbed his face. Fifty feet farther, the slope ended in a sheer drop. O'Leary crept close to the edge, looked down a vertical face that disappeared into mistiness.

"Splendid," he commented to the airy abyss. "Perfect. Fits right in with everything else that's happened. No wonder the old lady flew off on a broomless broom. Not even a fly could climb down that.

"So—I simply continue along the edge until I come to a road, path, or stairway leading down," he advised.

"You left out a rope ladder or a funicular railway.

"A regrettable omission. Eenie, Meenie, Miney, Mo . . . that way." He set off, following the cliff line. Another hour passed, the monotony of fatigue, pain, and frostbite broken only by two or three slips that almost pitched him over the edge.

"You're losing your stuff, O'Leary," he panted, struggling back to his feet after the last spill. "Just a few years ago, a little hike like this would have been child's play.

"Well, I can't expect to live in luxury, with every whim attended, and stay as hard as I was when I lived by my wits.

"There must be a lesson in that for me, but I hate to admit it."

The wind had increased; a driving downpour sluiced across the rock. O'Leary staggered on. His fingers and toes and lips were numb. He covered another half-mile before he paused for another conference.

"Something's bound to turn up soon," he told himself in tones of false confidence, rubbing his stiff fingers against his aching ears. "A footprint, or a dropped hanky, say . . ."

BEE-beep, BEE-beep, BEE-beep . . . The tiny sound seemed to be right beside him. Lafayette looked all around, saw nothing.

"Look here," he said aloud. "Talking to myself is bad enough, but in Morse code?"

He resumed rubbing his ears.

BEE-beep, BEE-beep, BEE-beep, the tone sounded sharply. O'Leary looked at his hands. Duke Rodolpho's ring winked on his middle finger. The ruby light glowed, dimmed, glowed, dimmed . . .

"Hey," O'Leary said weakly. He put the ring cautiously to his ear. It beeped steadily on in time with the flashing light.

"It didn't do that before," he told himself suspiciously.

"Well—it's doing it now," he came back smartly. "And it must have some significance.

"Maybe—maybe it's a radio beam—a beacon, like the airlines use.

"Maybe. Let's test it." He slogged downslope, fifty feet—listened again.

Bee-BEEP, bee-BEEP, bee-BEEP. . . .

"A-ha! That means I'm moving off course." He moved on, angling back upslope. Now the ring emitted a steady hum.

"On course," O'Leary breathed. "But on course for what?

"What does it matter? Anyplace would be better than here.

"True." Head down, his eyes squinted against the freezing rain, O'Leary plowed on, the ring held to his ear. The hum grew steadily louder. A clump of sodden stalks barred his way. He pushed through—and was teetering over empty space. For a wild instant he clutched at the sky for nonexistent support. Then the wind was blasting past him like a hurricane. The cliff face flashing upward like the shaft of an express elevator; O'Leary noticed the large 21 painted in white as it shot past; the 20; the 19, a mere blur—

From somewhere, a giant baseball bat swung, knocked him over the fence for a home run amid a vast display of Roman candles, while thousands cheered.

Seven

Someone had used his back as a diving board; or possibly they had mistaken it for a Persian rug and given it a good flailing with steel rods. His stomach had been employed by a gang of road menders for brewing up a batch of hot tar; he could distinctly feel the bubbles swelling and popping. His head had been dribbled up and down a basketball court for several close-fought quarters; and his eyes—apparently they'd been extracted, used in a Ping-Pong tournament, and rudely jammed back into their sockets.

"Hey—I think he's coming around," a frog-deep voice said. "That last groan was a lot healthier-sounding."

"He's all yours, Roy. Let me know if he relapses." Footsteps clunked; a door opened and closed. Lafayette pried an eye open, looked up at a perforated acoustical ceiling with flush-mounted fluorescents. Ignoring the fish spear someone had carelessly left embedded in his neck, he turned his head, saw a stubby little man with a cheerful, big-nosed face peering at him anxiously.

"How are ya, pal?" the watcher inquired.

"Yockabump," O'Leary chirped feebly, and lay back to watch the lights whirl.

"Cripes, a foreigner," the froggy voice said. "Sorry, Slim—me no spikka Hungarisha, you savvy?"

"But I guess you're not really Yockabump." O'Leary managed a thin whisper. "You just look like him, like everybody else in this nightmare looks like somebody they aren't."

"Hey, you can talk after all! Boy, you had me worried. I never lost a customer yet, but I came close today. You were in some rush, Slim—couldn't even wait for the elevator." The little man mopped at his face with a green-monogrammed red bandanna.

Lafayette's eyes roved around the room. It was ivory-walled, tile-floored. The soft susurrus of air-conditioning whispered from a grille above the door.

"What happened?" He tried to sit up, flopped back.

"Don't worry, Slim," the little man said. "The doc says you're O.K., just shook up."

"I . . . I seem to have a sort of confused memory," O'Leary said, "of stepping down an elevator shaft—out in the wilderness?"

"Yeah. Fell two floors. Lucky at that, no busted bones."

"Isn't that a rather peculiar location for an elevator shaft?"

The little man looked surprised. "How else you figure we're gonna get up and down? Hey, you ain't got in mind filing no claim against the company, I hope? I mean, I picked up your beep, and I was coming as fast as I could, right? You should of just held your horses."

"No doubt you're right. By the way—who are you?"

The little man thrust out a square, callused hand. "Sprawnroyal is the handle, Slim; Customer Service. Glad to make your acquaintance. You're a day early, you know. The order's not quite ready."

"Oh . . . the order," Lafayette temporized. "Frankly, I'm a little confused. By the fall, you know. Ah . . . what order was that?"

"Yeah, I guess you got a little concussion. Affects the memory." Sprawnroyal shook his heavy head sympathetically. "Your boss, Prince Krupkin, give us a down payment on a two-passenger rug, a blackout cloak, and a dozen illusions, the number-seventy-eight assortment."

"Oh, a two-passenger assortment and a dozen rugs," O'Leary mumbled. "Splendid. Ready tomorrow, you say?"

"You better lay here awhile and get it together, kid," Sprawnroyal advised. "Your brains is still a little scrambled."

"No—no, I'm fine." O'Leary sat up shakily. He had been bathed, he saw, and shaved and bandaged here and there and dressed in baggy pajamas—yellow with purple dots.

"By the way," he said. "How did you . . . ah . . . know I was here about the, ah, prince's order?"

Sprawnroyal blinked at him. "Who else would be wearing one of the tight-beam signalers we made up for him?"

"Of course, how could I forget a thing like that?" O'Leary swung his legs over the side of the bed and got to his feet. His knees wobbled but held.

"I just need a little fog to clear the exercise out of my head," he said. "I mean some head, to fog the clear . . . some clead. I mean the head—"

Sprawnroyal's hand grabbed for Lafayette's elbow. "Yeah. Take it easy, Slim. How's about some hot chow, hey? Good for what ails ya."

"Chow," Lafayette creaked. "Yes, by all means."

"Come on—if you're sure you can walk O.K." The little man handed him a bathrobe, led the way along a twisting corridor apparently cut from living rock and carpeted in pale nylon, into a low-ceilinged wood-paneled room with a long bar at one side backed by huge copper-bound kegs. At tables spread with checkered cloths other small, sturdily built men sat talking volubly over large coffee mugs. Several of them waved or nodded to O'Leary's guide as he steered him across to a table beside a curtained window beyond which rain swirled and beat against the glass. A jaw-aching aroma of fresh-ground coffee and fresh-baked bread filled the air. A plump little waitress with a turned-up nose, no taller than Lafayette's middle button, bustled over and slid cups in front of them, gave O'Leary a wink, and poised a pencil over her pad.

"What'll it be boys? Hotcakes? Steak and eggs? Strawberries and cream? Toast and jam and honey-butter?"

"Right," O'Leary said eagerly. "And a big glass of milk."

"Sounds good, Gert," Sprawnroyal said. "Me, too."

"Coming up."

Sprawnroyal rubbed his hands together, grinning. "Well, this is more like it, eh, Slim? Nothing like a snack to brighten the outlook."

"It's a distinct improvement over that." O'Leary indicated the dreary downpour outside. "There's just one little point that bothers me: where am I?"

"I don't get you, Slim. You're right here, at the Ajax Specialty Works, Melange Branch, having a midmorning snack in the Yggdrasil Room."

"Oh, in a factory. Well, that's a relief. Don't laugh, but I had the silly idea I was inside a cliff."

"Yeah, sure. But it wasn't always a cliff, understand. When the branch was first set up, it was under level ground. But there was the usual geological activity, and the plain subsided on us. But we got used to the split-level layout. And the view ain't bad."

"Geological activity?" Lafayette frowned. "You mean an earthquake?"

"Naw, just a spell of mountain-building. Happens every now and then, you know. Next time, this place may wind up under half a mile of seawater, you can't tell."

"O.K., move the elbows," Gert called, arriving with a laden tray. Lafayette managed to restrain himself until she laid out the food; then he pitched in with a will.

"Say, Slim," Sprawnroyal said with his mouth full. "How long you been on the prince's payroll?"

"Ah . . . not long," Lafayette said, chewing. "In fact, you might say no time at all."

"Say, just between the two of us—how's the old boy's credit rating holding up?"

"His credit?" Lafayette jammed his mouth full of hotcake and made incoherent sounds.

The Customer Service man held up a hand. "Not that we're worried, you understand," he said worriedly, "but he still owes us a bundle on the Glass Tree job."

Lafayette paused with his fork halfway to his mouth.

"Glass Tree job?" he mused. "Where have I heard of that before?"

"Say, Slim, you're *really* out of it."

"I've got an idea, Mr. Sprawnroyal," O'Leary said. "Why don't you just pretend that I haven't the faintest idea what's been happening, and just sort of fill me in? It will speed my recovery."

"Call me Roy. Well, where to start? We first hear from his Highness a few years back, when he drops around looking for a job. That was while he was still a commoner. He's got a few ideas, you know, so we put him to work in R & D. After a couple months the boss has to let him go. He's got the biggest light bill of anybody on the staff, but no production. The next we know, he's back flashing a fat purse and with a set of specs, wants to know can we knock out a few special-order items. We fix him up, he pays off in cut gemstones, and everybody's happy. Then he promotes himself to prince, and comes up with this construction job, wants to know if we'll take the contract. The price is right, so we go along. Do him a nifty job, too: the whole thing is formed-in-place silicone, microfiber-reinforced. A plush installation, believe you me."

"Yes—but where does this Glass Tree you mentioned come in?"

"That's what the construction-crew boys started calling it; the name caught on. Looks kind of like a tree at that, with all them turrets and minarets and stuff branching off the main keep. Shines real snazzy in the sun. Only it ain't paid for," Sprawnroyal finished on a glum note.

"Does this prince have an old lady on his payroll—one who flies on a broom—I mean without a broom?"

O'Leary's host eyed him solicitously. "Maybe you better go back and lay down, Slim—"

"Listen, Roy: last night an old lady mentioned the Glass Tree—just after she tried to kill me."

"Cripes! With a gun?"

"No. She—"

"Oh, used a knife, eh?"

"No, it was a vicious bare-handed attack—"

"While you were asleep, I bet!"

"Certainly not! But—"

"You *did* say an old lady?"

"Please, Roy—I'm trying to tell you—"

"Maybe you ought to go in for lifting, Slim, you know, weights. Get you in shape in no time, you wouldn't have to worry about no old ladies roughing you up. Now, I can make you a attractive price on our Atlas set number two-two-three, complete with a ear-link for pep talks and inspirational messages—"

"I don't need a pep talk! What I'm trying to say is, this old lady has something to do with the Lady Andragorre's disappearance!"

"Lady who?"

"Andragorre. She's my wife. I mean, she isn't

really my wife, but—"

"Oh, I get it." Sprawnroyal winked. "You can rely on my discretion, Slim."

"That's not what I meant! She's a very beautiful girl, and she disappeared on her way to a kidnapping. I mean she was kidnapped on her way to a disappearance. Anyway, she's gone! And the old bat at the hut mentioned the Glass Tree!"

"So? Well, I guess everybody in these parts would know about it." Sprawnroyal frowned. "The only thing is, there ain't nobody *in* these parts."

"The old woman must work for this Prince Krupkin! She mistook me for someone else—she's nearsighted, I guess—and let slip that she was expecting her Ladyship to be delivered to her at her hut!"

"I don't get it. If this old dame is on the prince's payroll same as you, how come she jumps you?"

"She thought I'd double-crossed her, led Duke Rodolpho's men to her."

"Chee—you know Duke Rodolpho? His Grace fired in a inquiry some time back, wanted quotes on a Personal Aura Generator; but we couldn't get together on price."

"The point is—this Krupkin fellow must be behind the kidnapping. Only something went wrong, and Lady Andragorre was snatched out from under his nose before the old lady could take delivery."

"This Lady A is from Rodolpho's duchy, huh?" Sprawnroyal shook his head. "It don't make sense, Slim. That's a long way out of his territory for a strong-arm play."

"He lured her out of town first—she thought

she was going to a rendezvous with some slicker named Lorenzo who'd insinuated himself into her good graces, not knowing the miserable sneak intended to hand her over to Krupkin." Lafayette rubbed the unbruised side of his face. "But who could have intercepted her?"

"Who indeed? It could of been anybody. The woods is full of cutpurses and footpads. Better forget it, Slim, and let's get back to business. Now, about that overdue payment—"

"Forget the most beautiful, wonderful, faithful, marvelous creature who ever wore a bikini? You don't seem to understand, Roy! At this very moment she may be in the most terrible danger— lonely, scared, maybe being tortured, or . . . or . . ."

"You said yourself she was on her way to a get-together with some guy name of Lorenzo, Slim," Sprawnroyal said in a reasonable tone, smearing jam on his third slice of golden-brown toast. "Looks like Krupkin's cut out of the pattern anyway, so why sweat it?"

"I told you, she was tricked!"

"Oh. You mean the guy told her he wanted her to look at some property, or take a test spin in a new model coach?"

"No, it was to be more of a trial honeymoon, as I understand it," O'Leary confessed. "But that's neither here nor there. Someone grabbed her, and I want to get her back!"

"How about this Lorenzo guy? You figure him for the snatch?"

"Well—I suppose he could have done it. Maybe he changed his mind at the last moment and couldn't go through with Krupkin's plan. In fact, the more I think of it, the likelier it seems. He probably abducted her from the coach as planned, and then instead of taking her to the hut, he took her . . . somewhere else.''

"Nice piece of deductive reasoning, Slim. So I guess the best man won—and they live happily ever after. Well, maybe not really the best man, who knows, maybe he's scared of old ladies too; what I mean is—''

"I know what you mean!" Lafayette snapped. "Listen, Roy: I have to find her!''

"I've got to admire your loyalty to your boss, Slim—but I'm afraid he'll have to line up something else—''

"To heck with my boss! Anyway, I may as well tell you: he's not my boss.''

"You mean—you quit?''

"I never worked for him. You leaped to a faulty conclusion. I'm sorry.''

"Then—where'd you get his signaler?''

"If you mean this ring—'' Lafayette held up the sparkling red stone. "Duke Rodolpho gave it to me.''

"Huh?'' Sprawnroyal grabbed O'Leary's finger and gave the gem a careful scrutiny.

"It's Krupkin's, all right.'' The little man lowered his voice. "On the level, Slim, what'd you do, slit his throat to get it?''

"Certainly not! I've never even seen the fellow!''

Sprawnroyal shook his head, his eyes hard on O'Leary. "It don't figure, Slim. How would the duke get the prince's ring? His Highness set a lot of store by that gimcrack—I know.''

"All I know is, the duke had it—and he gave it

to me." Lafayette tugged at the ring, slipped it over his knuckle. "Here," he said, "you can have it back. I don't want it. I'm only interested in finding Lady Andragorre."

His host weighed the ring on his palm, looking grim.

"Slim, you're in trouble," he said; he pushed back his chair. "Come on; you and me better go see Flimbert, our security chief, trial judge, one-man jury, and enforcer. He won't like this development at all, at all. And on the way you better think up a better story than the one you told me. Otherwise, I'm afraid we'll have to invoke the full rigor of Ajax Commercial Regulations."

"What does that mean?" O'Leary snapped. "You'll cut off my credit?"

"Not quite, Slim. More like your head."

Flimbert was a round-faced, hairless gnome with half-inch-thick lenses which looked as though they were permanently set in his head. He drummed his pudgy fingers on his desktop as Sprawnroyal gave his account of O'Leary's appearance. "I checked: the ring's one of the ones we made up for Prince Krupkin, all right," he finished.

"It looks like a clear case of murder and grand larceny, compounded by unauthorized entry, false pretenses, and perjury," Flimbert piped in a voice like a peanut whistle. "Any last words, you?" He looked at O'Leary like an angry goldfish peering through its bowl.

"Last words? I haven't even had my first ones yet! All I know is I was crawling along peacefully, minding my own business, when I fell down that lift shaft of yours! And I didn't say I was from Krupkin—that was Roy's idea. And where do you get that murder charge? Talk about conclusions of the witness—"

"Prince Krupkin would never have let his personal signaler out of his sight. Ergo, you must have killed him to get it. Open and shut. By the power vested in me—"

"I told you, I got the ring from Rodolpho!"

"Equally unlikely. Krupkin wouldn't have given it to Rodolpho either—"

"But he did! Why don't you check my story, instead of railroading me!"

"Hey, Bert," Roy said, rubbing his massive chin. "I been wondering: why would Slim here come up with a story as screwy as this unless it was true? And if he was trying to pull something, how come he told me himself he wasn't from Krupkin? He could've fooled me: the guy has a fantastic grasp of the prince's affairs."

"Hey," Lafayette protested.

"It's an old trick," the security chief said. "Reverse cunning, we call it in the security game; indistinguishable from utter stupidity."

"Welcome to the club," Lafayette said. "Look, Krupkin gave the ring to Rodolpho; Rodolpho gave it to me. I came here by accident, and all I want now is to leave—"

"Impossible. You've been caught red-handed, fellow. Unauthorized possession is the worst crime on the books. You're going to spend the next three hundred years chained to a treadmill in level twelve—"

"I'm afraid I'll have to disappoint you," Lafayette snapped. "I won't live three hundred years."

"Oh. Sorry, I didn't realize you were sick. We'll just make it a life sentence then; don't feel badly if you can't go the whole route."

"That's thoughtful of you. Say, just as a sort of intellectual exercise, why don't you spend thirty seconds or so considering the possibility that Rodolpho *did* have Krupkin's ring?"

"His Grace with his Highness's ring?" Flimbert put his fingertips together and looked grave. "Well, first, it would be a gross breach of the conditions of sale. Secondly, it would be quite unlike Krupkin, who never does anything without a good reason."

"So—he had a reason! Aren't you curious as to what the reason was?"

"I wonder." Sprawnroyal picked up the ring, held it to his nose, and studied it. "He couldn't've tinkered with it . . . ?"

"Nonsense; only a man trained in our own shops—" Flimbert broke off. "Now that you mention it, Krupkin *was* trained in our shops . . ."

"Yeah—and he's a top man, microengineeringwise," Sprawnroyal put in. "Cripes, but—could the guy have had a angle he was working?"

The security chief whipped out a jewelers' loupe, examined the ring.

"Just as I thought," he said crisply. "Tool marks." He laid the ring aside, poked a button on his desk. "Security to lab," he barked.

"Pinchcraft here," a testy voice responded. "What do you want, I'm in the midst of a delicate operation."

"Oh—the gnat-borne miniaturized-TV-camera project?"

"No, I was fishing the olive out of my martini with a paper straw. I almost had it when you made me jiggle it!"

"Forget the olive; I'm on my way down with a little item I want you to take a look at before I carry out the death sentence on a spy!"

The laboratory was a rough-hewn cavern crowded with apparatus as complex and incomprehensible to O'Leary as a Chinese joke book. They found the research boss perched on a high stool before a formica-topped bench poking at a glittering construction of coils and loops of glass tubing through which pink and green and yellow fluids bubbled, violet vapors curled.

Security Chief Flimbert handed over the ring. The research chief spun on his stool, snapped on a powerful light, flipped out a magnifying lens, bent over the ring.

"A-ha," he said. "Seal's broken." He pursed his lips, gave O'Leary a sharp look. With a needle-pointed instrument, he prodded the bezel of the ruby, flipped open a tiny cover, revealing an interior hollow packed with intricate components.

"Well, well," he said. "Haven't we been a busy boy?" He put the ring down and quickly placed an empty coffee cup over it.

"Find somethin'?" Roy asked anxiously.

"Nothing much—just that the entire device has been rewired," Pinchcraft snapped. "It's been

rigged to act as a spy-eye." He glared at O'Leary.
"What did you hope to learn? Our trade secrets?
They're freely available to the public: hard work
and common sense."

"Don't look at me," O'Leary said. "I haven't
tampered with it."

"Uh—the ring was made up for Prince Krupkin," Roy pointed out.

"Krupkin, eh? Never did trust that jumped-up
jack-in-office. Sneaky eyes."

"Yeah—but Slim here says he didn't get the
bauble from Krupkin. He claims it was given to
him by Duke Rodolpho."

"Nonsense. I remember this order now: I designed the circuits myself, in accordance with
Krupkin's specs. Yes, and now I see why he insisted there be no modifications! The thing was
shrewdly designed for easy conversion. All he
had to do was switch the A wire to ground, the B
wire to contact A, the C wire to contact D, reverse
wires D and E, shunt wire F off to resistance X, and
throw in the odd little black box. Nothing to it."

"I still got it from Rodolpho," Lafayette said
hotly. "He gave it to me as a safe-conduct for a
mission I undertook for him."

"You'll have to think up a better story," Flimbert said. "That ring wouldn't get you through a
schoolboy patrol line."

"Say," Roy put in, "maybe he meant to give you
the ducal signet—I saw him wearing it when we
were dickering. It's got a ruby, too, with a big RR
carved on it. Maybe he grabbed the wrong one.
How was the light?"

"Wet, as I recall," Lafayette aid. "Look, gentlemen, we're wasting time. Now that the misun-

derstanding is cleared up, if I could have my clothes back, I'll be on my way—"

"Not so fast, you!" Pinchcraft said. "We have methods of dealing with those who renege on the solemn fine print in a contract!"

"Then see Krupkin, he's the one who signed it."

"He has a point," Pinchcraft said. "Krupkin, as contracting party, is ultimately responsible. This fellow is merely an accessory."

"What's the penalty for that?"

"Much less severe," Flimbert said grudgingly. "Only one hundred years on the treadmill."

"Hey, that's a break, hey, Slim?" Roy congratulated him.

"I'm overwhelmed," Lafayette said. "Look, fellows, couldn't we work something out? A suspended sentence, maybe?"

"Hey, maybe we could give him a feat to perform," Roy proposed. "We got a couple lines of hand-painted neckties that ain't been moving. Maybe he could go on the road with 'em—"

"This is all wrong!" O'Leary protested. "Krupkin is the one behind this—I'm just an innocent bystander. And I think he's also behind the Lady Andragorre's kidnapping."

"That's no concern of ours."

"Maybe not—but I thought you had dire penalties for anybody who tinkered with your products."

"Hmmm." Flimbert fingered his nose. "We do, at that."

"Listen," O'Leary said urgently. "If Krupkin could convert a personal signaler to a spy-eye, why couldn't you rewire the ring to reverse the action?"

"Eh?"

"Rig it so that instead of relaying sounds from the vicinity of the ring back to Krupkin, it would transmit sounds from Krupkin to you."

Pinchcraft frowned. "Possibly. Possibly." He signaled for silence, lifted the cup. Holding the ring in the light, he went to work. The others watched silently as he probed inside the case, murmuring, ". . . wire B to Contact D . . . conductor E to remitter X . . . red . . . blue . . . green . . . ." After ten minutes, he said "Ha!," closed the back of the ring, and held it to his ear. He smiled broadly.

"I can hear him," he said. "No doubt this ring is tuned to its twin, which Krupkin keeps on his person." He handed the ring to Flimbert.

"Ummm. That's his voice, all right."

"Well—what's he saying?" O'Leary demanded.

"He's singing. Something about a road to Mandalay."

"Let me listen." Flimbert gave him the ring; he held it to his ear: ". . . *Bloomin' idol made of mu-ud . . . what they called the great god Buddd . . .*" The words came indistinctly through the sound of running water. Lafayette frowned. The voice seemed to have a half-familiar note. Abruptly, the singing cut off. Lafayette heard a faint tapping, followed by a muttered curse, footsteps, the sound of a door opening.

"Well?" the voice that had been singing said testily.

"Highness . . . the pris—that is to say, your guest declines to join you for breakfast—with, ah, appropriate apologies, of course."

"Blast the wench, can't she see I'm trying to

make her comfortable, nothing more? And don't
bother lying to me, Haunch. That little baggage
doesn't know the meaning of the word 'apology.'
She's done nothing but stamp her foot and make
demands since the moment she arrived. I tell you,
there are times when I wonder if it's worth all the
maneuvering involved, trying to set up shop as a
benevolent despot."

"Shall I, er, convey your Highness's invitation
to lunch?"

"Don't bother, just see that she has whatever
she wants served in her room. Keep her as content
as possible. I don't want her developing frown
lines or chapped knuckles while in my care."

"Of course, Highness." Footsteps, a closing
door; a few bars of under-the-breath whistling;
then sudden silence, with heavy breathing.

"Damn!" the voice muttered. "Could those
little—?" The voice broke off. There were loud,
rasping sounds, then a dull *clunk!* followed by
total silence.

"Oh-oh," Lafayette aid. "He's stopped trans-
mitting."

The others listened in turn. "He must have
realized something was amiss," Pinchcraft said.
"Probably stuffed the ring in a box and closed the
lid. So much for counterintelligence."

"Too bad," O'Leary said brightly. "Just as it was
getting interesting."

"Yes; well, let's be going, fellow," Flimbert
said. "The treadmill is waiting."

"Well—good-bye, Roy," O'Leary said. "I
wouldn't want to default on my debt to society, of

course—but I certainly will hate missing all the excitement."

"Oh, life around the Ajax Works is pretty quiet, Slim; you won't be missing much."

"Just the invasion," Lafayette said. "It ought to be quite spectacular when Krupkin arrives with his army, navy, and air force."

"What's that?" Flimbert snapped. "What are you talking about?"

"Oh—I forgot I was the only one who heard him. But never mind. Maybe he was only fooling."

"Who?"

"Prince Krupkin. He was closeted with his War Cabinet, laying on the strategy for the takeover. He cut off just as he was about to announce the timetable for the three-pronged assault."

"Nonsense! Krupkin wouldn't attack Ajax!"

"Probably not. Just his idea of a joke. Of course, he didn't know we were listening—but then maybe he's an eccentric and was just reading off logistical schedules for the fun of it."

"He couldn't be so base as to use our own equipment against us?" Flimbert inquired, aghast.

"I wouldn't put it past him!" Pinchcraft said.

"Well, I'd better get started treading that mill," Lafayette said. "You gentlemen will be pretty busy for the next twenty-four hours, I suppose, making out wills and burying your valuables—"

"Just a moment. What else did he say? When does he plan to hit us? How many troops has he under arms? What will his primary objectives be?

What kind of armaments—"

"Sorry, that was the part he was just coming to."

"Drat it! Why couldn't we have tuned in sooner!"

"Look here—can't you rig up something else, Pinchcraft?" Flimbert demanded. "We have to know what's going on over there!"

"Not without a pickup planted at that end, I can't."

"What about sending over a robot bird to scatter a few bugs around the premises?"

"Useless. The range on these micro-micro jobs is very short. The pickup has to be planted on or near the person of the subject to do us any good."

"We'll have to send a man in."

"Nonesense. None of our boys are as tall as those beanpoles; anyone we sent would be spotted instantly. Unless—"

All eyes turned to O'Leary.

"What, me stick my head in the lions' den?" he said with raised eyebrows. "Not a chance. I'm on my way to a nice, safe treadmill, remember?"

"Now, now, my boy," Flimbert said with a smile like the father of a pauper's bride, "don't worry about the treadmill. You can always serve out your sentence after you get back—"

"Forget the sentence," Pinchcraft said. "This is more important. Don't you want to do your bit, fellow, to assist the forces of righteousness?"

"What have the forces of righteousness done for me lately?" O'Leary inquired rhetorically. "No, thanks, men, you can just carry on without me as you did before I came along."

"See here, Slim" Roy said. "I didn't think you

were the kind of fellow who'd let the side down when the pinch came."

"The pinch came half an hour ago, remember? You did the pinching."

"Sir," Pinchcraft spoke up, "we appeal to your nobler instincts! Assist us now, and earn our undying gratitude!"

O'Leary patted back a yawn. "Thanks—I'm overstocked on gratitude."

"Possibly some more negotiable form of payment . . . ?" Flimbert suggested.

O'Leary raised an eyebrow, pursed his lips.

"You'll have the best equipment from our labs," Pinchcraft said quickly. "I'm just finishing up a blackout cloak in your size, as it happens, and—"

"We'll drop you onto a balcony on the main turret of the Glass Tree on a fast one-place rug," Flimbert chimed in. "The trip won't take an hour."

"Are you out of your minds?" O'Leary demanded. "My only chance would be to sneak up after dark and try for an unlocked door."

"Not with this on!" Pinchcraft hopped from his stool, grabbed up a long, red-lined green-velvet cape from a worktable, and swirled it around himself. The heavy fabric whirled, shimmered—and disappeared, along with the small technician.

"Huh?" O'Leary said.

"Not bad, eh?" Pinchcraft's voice spoke from the emptiness where he had stood a moment before.

"M-magic?" Lafayette stuttered.

"Nonsense. Electronics." Pinchcraft's face appeared, framed by nothingness. "Well, how about it?"

O'Leary forced the astounded look from his face.

"Well—I might go," he said, "provided you make that a two-man rug."

"Whatever you want, Slim" Roy spoke up. "For a volunteer hero like you, nothing but the best!"

"Don't worry, we'll get you in," Pinchcraft said.

"And out again?" O'Leary countered.

"One thing at a time," Flimbert said. "Come along, fellow, let's get you fitted out. I want you inside the Glass Tree by sundown."

Eight

It was late afternoon, Lafayette saw, when Sprawnroyal led him along a twisting passage to a double door opening on a tiny balcony overlooking the vast sweep of the valley below.

"Now, you want to be careful of the carpet, Slim" the Customer Relations man said as he rolled out the six-by-eight-foot rectangle of what looked like ordinary dark-blue Wilton carpet. "The circuits are tuned to your personal emanations, so nobody can hijack her. She's voice-operated, so be careful what you say. And remember, there's no railings, so watch those banked turns. The coordination's built in, naturally, but if you're careless—well, keep in mind you've got no parachute."

"That's all very encouraging," Lafayette said, adjusting the hang of the blackout cloak and fighting down a quivering sensation in his stomach. "With all this gear Pinchcraft loaded on me, I feel as maneuverable as a garbage scow."

"Frankly, he sees this as a swell chance to field-test a lot of the offbeat items he and his boys cook up on those long winter nights. Like the sneeze generator: top management wouldn't let him call for volunteers, even. And the flatwalker: it's a dandy idea, but if it doesn't work—*blooie!* There goes your research worker and a big chunk of lab."

"Fill me in with a little more data, and the flight is off," O'Leary said. "Just point me in the right direction before common sense overwhelms my instinct for making mistakes."

"Just steer due west, Slim. You can't miss it."

"You'd be amazed at some of the things I've missed," Lafayette said. "By the way, my name's not really Slim, you know. It's Lafayette O'Leary."

"Yeah? Say, that's a coincidence—but never mind that. Bon voyage, kid, and don't forget to flip the switch before you drop the bug in the target's pocket."

"Well," Lafayette said, easing into a sitting position on the dark rug, legs folded. "Here goes . . ."

He closed his eyes, thought about the coordinates Flimbert had drilled him in for half an hour. Under him, the thick wool nap seemed to vibrate minutely. He reisisted an impulse to grab for support as the rug stirred, twitched, tightened; forced himself to sit limply.

"Like a sack of potatoes," he reminded himself while sweat ran down behind his head. "A big burlap bag of good old Idaho baking potatoes . . ."

The tugging, swaying sensation went on; a breeze that had sprung up blew gustily at him, riffling his hair, making the cloak flap.

"Come on, lift!" he hissed. "Before that Flimbert sharpy realizes they've been conned!"

Nothing changed. The wind whipped briskly about him; the rug felt passive under him.

"Oh, great," Lafayette said. "I should have known this idea wouldn't work." He opened his eyes gazed blankly for a moment at the vista of open blue sky ahead, then turned, looked back. . . .

On the tiny balcony scabbed to the face of the immense cliff receding rapidly behind him, a tiny figure waved a scarf. O'Leary forced his eyes down, saw the rolling grassy landscape sliding swiftly behind him. He closed his eyes tightly.

"Mamma mia," he muttered. "And me without even a paper bag, in case I get airsick!"

The palace-fortress known as the Glass Tree rose out of the west like a star caught on the peak of a mountain. Dazzling in the rays of the setting sun, it scintillated red and green and yellow and violet, materializing gradually into a cluster of sparkling, crystalline shafts. A branching structure of tall towers, dazzling bright minarets, glittering spires, clustered on the tip of the highest peak of the range.

"O.K., cloak, do your stuff," O'Leary murmured, gathering the garment about him, arranging the wide skirts so as to encompass as much as possible of the carpet itself. Sprawnroyal had assured him that Prince Krupkin was in possession of no antiaircraft facilities, but Lafayette nonetheless scrunched down on the rug to provide the minimum possible target as he swooped toward the looming structure ahead.

At half a mile he ordered the rug to slow. If there was any change in the speed—too fast—and the direction—dead at the tallest tower—Lafayette was unable to detect it. With frightening speed, the slim, glittering minaret rushed closer. . . .

At the last possible instant, the rug braked, banked—almost pitching a petrified O'Leary over the side—and circled the tower.

"Like a sack of Idaho number-ones," O'Leary whispered urgently to himself. "Please, up there, just let me get out of this one alive, and I promise to tithe regularly. . . ."

The rug slewed to a halt, hung quivering in the air before a tall, Moorish-arched window.

"OK, all ahead, dead slow," Lafayette whispered. The rug drifted closer to the translucent, mirror-polished wall. When it nudged the crystal rail, he reached cautiously, grabbed, and held on. The rug bobbled and swayed under him as he climbed over; relieved of his weight, it began to drift away, rippling slightly in the breeze. Lafayette caught a corner, pulled the carpet to him, rolled it into a tight cylinder, and propped it in a corner.

"Just wait here until I get back," he whispered to it. He took a moment to tuck in the tail of the embroidered shirt Sprawnroyal had supplied, and tug his jeweled sword into line, then pressed the button set in the pommel of the latter.

"Flapjack to Butterfly," he whispered. "O.K., I'm down, in one piece."

"Very good," a shrill whisper rasped from the two-way comm rig installed in the weapon's hilt. "Proceed inside, and make your way to the royal apartments. They're on the twelfth floor of the main keep. Watch your step; don't give yourself *away by knocking over a vase or stepping on somebody's foot."*

"Glad you mentioned that," Lafayette snapped. "I intended to come on strumming a ukulele and singing 'Short'nin' Bread.' "

He tried the door, stepped into a dim-lit, softly carpeted chamber hung with rose-and-silver drapes. A pink- and silver four-poster stood opposite the balcony. Silver cupids disported themselves at the corners of the dusty-rose ceiling. A wide crystal chandelier sparkled in the center of the room, tinkling with the breeze from the open door. Lafayette started toward a wide silver-and-white door at the far side of the room, halted at the sound of voices beyond it.

". . . just for a nightcap," a wheedling male voice said. "And besides," it went on with an audible leer, "you might need a little help with those buttons."

"You're impertinent, sir," a familiar feminine voice said in a playful tone. "But I suppose it will be all right—for a few minutes."

"Daphne?" Lafayette mumbled. As a key clattered in the lock, he dived for the shelter of the four-poster. He had no more than gained the darkness behind the brocaded skirt when the door opened. Lying with his face to the rug, Lafayette could see a pair of trim ankles in tiny black patent-leather pumps with silver buckles, closely attended by a pair of shiny black boots with jingling jeweled spurs. The two sets of feet moved across the room, out of Lafayette's line of sight. There were soft sounds as of gentle scuffling, a low laugh.

"Avaunt thee, sirrah!" the female voice said mildly. "You'll muss my coiffure."

As Lafayette stretched to get a glimpse of the action from behind the carved claw-and-ball foot of the bed, his sword clanked against the floor. Instantly there was silence.

"Milord Chauncy—didst hear that?"

"Well, I really must be going," the male voice said loudly, with a slight quaver. "As you know, his Highness—the best boss a fellow ever had— gave orders you were to have whatever you wanted, milady—but I'm afraid that if I lingered any longer attending to your whims, it might be susceptible of misinterpretation—"

"Why, of all the nerve!" There was a sharp *smack!* as of a wrathful feminine hand striking an arrogant male cheek. "As if I invited you here!"

"So . . . if you'll excuse me—"

"Not until you've searched the room! It might be a horrid big bristly rat!"

"Yes, but—"

A dainty foot stamped. "At once, Chauncy, or I'll report that you tried to force your lustful will on me!"

"Who, me, your Ladyship?"

"You heard me!"

"Well . . ." Lafayette saw the boots cross the room, pause before the closet; the door opened and shut. The feet went on to the bathroom, disappeared inside, reemerged. They went to the balcony, stepped out, came back.

"Nothing at all. Probably just your imagination—"

"You heard it too! And you haven't looked under the bed!"

Lafayette froze as the feet crossed to the bed, halted two feet from the tip of his nose. The skirt was lifted; a narrow face with fierce, spiked mustachios and a pair of small, beady eyes peered directly into his face.

"Nothing here," the man said and let the skirt drop. Lafayette let out a breath he hadn't noticed he was holding. "Sure, I forgot the cloak," he chided himself.

"That being the case," the male voice continued, "what's my rush?"

"Art related to an octopus on thy father's side?" the Daphne-like voice was inquiring with a suppressed giggle. "Aroint thee, milord, thou'll break the zipper."

"Why, you . . ." Lafayette muttered, and froze as conversation again cut off abruptly.

"Chauncy—there's someone here!" the feminine voice said. "I . . . I sense it!"

"Yes, well, as I was saying, I have my sheet-and-towel inventory to check over, so I really can't linger—"

"Pooh, Chauncy, at this hour? Surely you're not afraid?"

"Me? Afraid?" Chauncy's voice broke on the word. "Of course not, it's just that I've always loved inventories, and this is my chance to steal a march by working on it all night, so—"

"Chauncy—we were going to take a moonlight walk, remember? Just you and me . . ."

"Yes, well—"

"Just wait while I slip into something more comfortable. Now, don't go 'way . . ."

"Hey," Lafayette murmured weakly.

"The acoustics in this room are terrible,"

Chauncy said nervously. "I would have sworn someone whispered 'hey' just then."

"Silly boy," the other voice replied. There was a soft rustling sound, followed by a sharp intake of masculine breath. The feminine feet reappeared; they paused before the closet; slim, ringed fingers appeared, to pull off one shoe, then the other. The feet went to tiptoe, and a voluminously skirted garment collapsed on the floor. A moment later, a filmy nothing floated down beside the dress.

"Really, milady," Chauncy's voice squeaked, "his Highness . . . but to perdition with his Highness!" The booted feet rushed across the floor, trod on a small, bare foot. There was a sharp yelp, followed by the second sharp *smack!* of the evening.

"You big, clumsy idiot!" the female voice wailed. "I'd rather stay cooped up here forever than put up with—"

"Oh, so that was your scheme, you slick little minx!" Chauncy cried. "You inveigled me here with promise of goodies to come—planning all the while to dupe me into abetting your escape! Well, this is one time the old skin game won't work, milady! I'm collecting right now—"

Lafayette emerged from under the bed in a rush. As he leaped to his feet, the owner of the boots—a tall, lean, courtier type in the pre-middle-aged group—spun, grabbing for his sword hilt, staring wildly over, past, and through O'Leary. Behind Chauncy, Daphne—or Lady Andragorre—bare-shouldered in a petticoat, stood on one shapely leg, massaging the toes of the other foot. Lafayette reached out, lifted the man's chin to the optimum angle, and delivered a sizzling right hook which sent the fellow staggering back to bounce off the wall and pitch forward on his face.

"Chauncy!" the lady whispered, watching his trajectory. "What—how—why—?"

"I'll teach that lecher to sneak around ladies' bedrooms helping them with their buttons," Lafayette said, advancing on the half-clad girl. "And as for you, I'm ashamed of you, leading that gigolo on!"

"I hear your voice . . . oh, beloved—I can hear you—but I can't see you! Where are you? You're not . . . you're not a ghost?"

"Far from it!" Lafayette pulled the cloak back from his face. "I'm flesh and blood, all right, and all I have to say about this spectacle is—"

The lady stared for a moment into O'Leary's face; then her eyes turned up. With a sigh, she crumpled onto the old rose rug.

"Daphne!" Lafayette blurted. "Wake up! I forgive you! But we have to get out of here in a hurry!" As O'Leary bent over her, there was a thunderous pounding at the door.

"There's a man in there!" an irate voice yelled from outside. "All right, men—break it down!"

"Hold your horses, Sarge—I got a key—"

"You heard me!" There was a thunderous crash that shook the door in its frame, the sound of heavy bodies rebounding.

"So, OK, we use the key." Lafayette slipped his arms under the unconscious girl and lifted her, staggered to the heavy hangings against the wall, and slid behind them as the lock clicked, the latch turned, the door banged wide. Three large men in cerise coats with lace at wrist and chin, tight cream-colored pants, and drawn swords plunged into the room and skidded to a halt.

They stared, then cautiously prowled the room.

"Hey! The place is empty," a man said.

"There's ain't nobody here," a second added.

"Yeah, but we heard voices, remember?"

"So we made a mistake."

"Either that, or . . ."

"Or we're all going crackers."

"Or else the joint is haunted."

"Well, I got to be getting back to my pinochle game," a private said, backing toward the door.

"Stand fast, you," the NCOIC barked. "I'll say when we get back to the pinochle game!"

"Yeah? You want to wait around and shake hands with the Headless Hostler?"

"And like you said, it's time we was getting back to the pinochle game," the sergeant finished sternly. "Let's go."

Three sets of footsteps retreated cautiously toward the door. As they reached it, Lafayette, standing behind the curtain inhaling the perfume of the girl in his arms, heard a preliminary crackle from his sword hilt.

"Oh, no," he breathed.

"*Butterfly to Flapjack,*" a testy voice sounded from near his left elbow. "*What's going on, Flapjack? You haven't reported for over five minutes now!*"

"Over there," a tense voice said. "Behind them drapes."

"*Flapjack? Report!*"

"Shut up, you blabbermouth!" Lafayette hissed in the general direction of his left hip, and sidestepped as the curtains were rudely torn aside.

"Chee!" the man who stood there said, staring wide-eyed at Lafayette's burden.

"Coo," said the comrade peering over his shoulder, and ran a thick pink tongue along his lower lip like one recovering a crumb of icing.

"Holy Moses," said the third. "She's . . . she's floating in midair, like!"

"She—she got little teeny rosebuds embroidered on her undies," the first man said. "Think o' that, fellers!"

"Walking or floating, them are the neatest curves a guy ever seen," his comrade stated.

"Hey—she's floating toward the balcony doors, boys!" a man blurted as O'Leary edged sideways. "Block the way!"

As the three palace guards spread out, O'Leary tried a play around left end, gained two yards, delivered a sharp kick to a kneecap as the owner reached a tentative hand toward milady's dangling arm. He dodged aside as the fellow yelled and clutched at the injured member, hopping on one foot. For the moment, the way to the door was clear; Lafayette lunged, felt the cloak tug at his back as the hopper trod on the hem; before he could halt his plunge, it was ripped from his back.

"Hey! A guy! He just popped out o' the air, like!" a man yelled. "Take him, Renfrew!" Lafayette made a desperate leap, ducked the haymaker, felt hard hands grab his ankles, saw other hands seize the girl as he went down, banging his head against the baseboard. Half-dazed, he was dragged to his feet and flung against the wall.

"Well, look who's here," the grinning face hovering before him said in tones of pleased surprise as hands slapped his pockets, relieving him of the gadgets pressed on him by Pinchcraft. "You get around, bub. But you should of thought twice before you tried this one, which his Nibs ain't going to like it much, you in here with her Lady-ship, and her in the altogether!"

"She's not altogether in the altogether," O'Leary mumbled, attempting to focus his eyes. "She's wearing her rosebuds."

"Hey, look!" another of the new arrivals called. "Lord Chauncy's over here back o' the divan! Boy oh boy, will you look at the size o' the mouse on his jaw!"

"Add assaulting his Lordship to the charges on this joker," the sergeant in charge said. "Kid, you should of stayed where you was. You didn't know when you was well off."

Two men were holding Lafayette's arms. The third had placed the unconscious girl on the bed.

"O.K., Mel, don't stand back to admire your work," the N.C.O. growled. "Let's hustle this joker back to the cell block before somebody finds out he's gone and starts criticizing the guard force."

"Can't I . . . can't I just say a word to her?" O'Leary appealed as his captors hustled him past the bed.

"Well—what the heck, kid, I guess you paid for the privilege. Make it fast."

"Daphne," Lafayette said urgently as her eyelids quivered, opened. "Daphne! Are you all right?"

For a moment, the girl looked dazedly around. Her eyes fell on Lafayette.

"Lancelot?" she whispered. "Lancelot . . . dearest . . ."

"OK, let's go," the NCO growled. Lafayette stared despairingly back as they escorted him from the room.

Nine

Lafayette sat in pitch darkness, slumped against a damp stone wall, shivering. The tomblike silence was broken only by the soft rustlings of mice frisking in the moldy straw and the rasp of heavy breathing from the far corner of the dank chamber. His fellow prisoner had not wakened when he was thrown into the cell, nor in the gloomy hours since. The aroma of Moonlight Rose still lingered in O'Leary's nostrils, in spite of the goaty stench of the dungeon. The memory of those soft, warm contours he had held briefly in his arms sent renewed pangs through him every time he let his thoughts rove back over the events since his arrival at the Glass Tree.

"I really handled it brilliantly," he muttered. "I had every break—even stumbled right into her room, first try—and I still muffed it. I've done everything wrong since the second I found myself perched on the windmill. I've let down everybody, from Swinehild to Rodolpho to Pinchcraft, not to mention Daph—I mean Lady Andragorre." He got to his feet, took the four paces his exploration of the dark chamber had indicated were possible before bumping a wall, paced back.

"There's got to be something I can do!" he hissed to himself. "Maybe . . ." He closed his eyes—an action which made very little difference under the circumstances—and concentrated his psychic energies.

"I'm back in Artesia," he muttered. "I've just stepped outside for a breath of air in the midst of a costume ball—that's why I'm wearing this fancy outfit Sprawnroyal gave me—and in a second or two I'll open my eyes and go back inside, and . . ."

His words trailed off. With the stench of the cell in his nostrils, it was impossible to convince himself that he was strolling in a garden where nothing more odiferous than a gardenia was to be found.

"Well, then—I'm inspecting the slums," he amended "—except that there aren't any slums in Artesia," he recalled. "But how about Colby Corners? We had a swell little slum back there, created and maintained by as determined a crew of slum dwellers as ever put coal in a bathtub." He squinted harder, marshaling his psychic forces. "I'm in a Federal Aid to Undesirables project," he assured himself, "doing research for a book on how long it takes the average family of ne'er-do-wells to convert a clean, new, modern welfare-supplied apartment into the kind of homey chaos they're used to . . ."

"Say, would you mind hallucinating a little more quietly?" a querulous voice with an edge like a gnawed fingernail inquired from the far corner of the room. "I'm trying to catch a few winks."

"Oh, so you're alive after all," Lafayette replied.

"I certainly admire your ability to doss down in comfort in the midst of this mare's nest."

"What do you suggest?" came the snappish reply. "That I huddle here with every nerve a-tingle to monitor each nuance of total boredom and discomfort?"

"How do we get out?" Lafayette said tersely. "That's the question we ought to be thinking about."

"You're good at questions, how are you at answers?" The voice, O'Leary thought, was a nerve-abrading combination of petulant arrogance and whining self-pity. He suppressed the impulse to snap back.

"I've tried the door," he said in tones of forced optimism. "It's a single slab of cast iron, as far as I can determine, which seems to limit the possibilities in that direction."

"You're not going to let a little thing like a cast-iron door slow you down, surely? From your tone of voice, I assumed you'd just twist it off its hinges and hit someone over the head with it."

". . . which means we'll have to look for some other mode of egress," O'Leary finished, gritting his teeth.

"Splendid. You work at that. As for me, I'm catching up on my sleep. I've had a pretty strenuous forty-eight hours—"

"Oh, have you? Well, it can't begin to compare with my last forty-eight hours. I started off on top of a windmill, worked my way through a homicidal giant and a set of pirates, two jail cells, an execution, a fall down an elevator shaft, a trial for espionage, and a trip on a flying carpet, to say nothing of the present contretemps."

"Uuuum-ha!" Lafayette's cellmate yawned. "Lucky you. As for myself, I've been busy: I've parlayed with a mad prince, dickered with a duke, carried out a daring rescue, double-crossed a sorcerer, and been beaten, kicked, hit on the head, slugged, and thrown in a dungeon."

"I see. And what are you doing about it?"

"Nothing. You see, it's actually all a dream. After a while I'll wake up and you'll be gone, and I can get back to my regular routine."

"Oh, I see. The solitude has driven you off your hinge. Rather ironic, actually," he added with a hollow chuckle. "You, imagining I'm a figment of your nightmare. I remember when I had similar ideas about a lot of things that turned out to be painfully real."

"So if you'll stop chattering, so I can go back to sleep, I'll be grateful," the abrasive voice remarked.

"Listen to me, Sleeping Beauty," O'Leary said sharply. "This is real—as real as anything that ever happened to you. Maybe hardship has driven you out of whatever wits you may once have had, but try to grasp the concept: you're in a cell—a real, live, three-dee cell, complete with mice. And unless you want to stay here until you rot—or the hangman comes for you—you'd better stir your stumps!"

"Go 'way. I haven't finished my nap."

"Gladly—if I could! Wake up, numbskull! Maybe between the two of us we can do something!"

"Poo. You're nothing but a figment. All I have to do is go back to sleep, and I'll wake up back in

Hatcher's Crossroads, bagging groceries at Bowser's."

Lafayette laughed hollowly. "You remind me of a poor innocent nincompoop I used to know," he said. "By the way, where's this Hatcher's Crossroads located?"

"In the Oklahoma Territory. But you wouldn't know about that. It's not part of this dream."

"Oklahoma—you mean you're from the States?"

"Oh, so you do know about the States? Well, why not! I suppose in theory you could know anything I know, eh? Well, ta-ta, I'm off to dreamland again—"

"Wait a minute," O'Leary said urgently. "Are you saying you were brought here from the U.S.? That you're not a native of Melange?"

"The U.S.? What's that? And of course I'm not a native. Do I look as though I'd run around in a G-string, waving an assegai?"

"I don't know, I can't see in the dark. But if you come from Oklahoma, you must know what the U.S. is!"

"You don't mean the U.C.?"

"What's that?"

"The United Colonies, of course. But look, be a good imaginary character and let me catch a few winks now, all right? This was all rather lark at first, but I'm getting tired of it, and I have a hard day ahead tomorrow. Mr. Bowser's running a special on pickled walnuts, and the whole county will be there—"

"Try to get this through your thick skull," Lafayette snarled. "You're here, in Melange, like it or not! It's real—whatever real is! If they hang you or cut your head off, you suffer the consequences, get it? Now, look, we have to talk about this. It sounds as if you were shanghaied here the same way I was—"

"I never knew my subconscious could be so persuasive. If I didn't know you were just a subjective phenomenon, I'd swear you were real."

"Look, let's skip that part for now. Just act as if I were real. Now, tell me: how did you get here?"

"Easy. A troop of Prince Krupkin's cavalry grabbed me by the back of the neck and threw me in here. Satisfied?"

"I mean before that—when you first arrived—"

"Oh, you mean when I focused the cosmic currents?" Lafayette's cellmate laughed hollowly. "If I'd known what I was getting into, I'd have stuck to my tinned kippers and jelly doughnuts. But no, I had to go intellectually questing, searching for the meaning of it all. And then I had the bad luck to stumble on Professor Hozzleshrumphs's book, *Modern Spellbinding, or Self-Delusion Made Easy.* I tried out his formulae, and—well, one second I was in my room at Mrs. Ginsberg's, and the next—I was in the middle of a vast desert, with the sun glaring in my face."

"Yes? Go on."

"Well, I started hiking east—that way the sun wasn't in my eyes—and after a while I reached the hills. It was cooler there, and I found a stream, and some nuts and berries. I kept on, and came out in a tilled field, near a town. I found a lunch counter, and just as I was about to take my first bite of grilled Parmesan cheese on rye, the local police force arrived. They took me in to the prince, and he offered me a job. It all seemed pretty jolly, so I went along. I was doing all right, too—until I got a look at the Lady Andragorre."

"Lady Andragorre? What do you know about Lady Andragorre?" Lafayette barked.

"I have to keep reminding myself this is just a dream" the unseen voice said agitatedly. "Otherwise, I'd be tearing my hair out!" Lafayette heard a deep breath drawn and let slowly out. "But it's all a dream, an illusion. Beverly really isn't in the clutches of that slimy little Krupkin; I haven't really been double-crossed and thrown in a cell. These aren't real hunger pangs I feel. And if you'd just shut up and go away, I could get back to my career at Bowser's!"

"Let's get back to Lady Andragorre!"

"Wouldn't I love to? Those sweet, soft lips, that curvey little frame—"

"Why, you—" Lafayette caught himself. "Listen to me, whoever you are! You've got to face up to reality! You have to help me! Right now Lady Andragorre's in the hands of these lechers—and I do mean hands—"

"Just last week Mr. Bowser was saying to me: Lorenzo, my boy, you have a great future ahead in the provisions game . . ."

"Lorenzo! Then you're the one that sold out Lady Andragorre!" Lafayette lunged in the direction from which the voice came, slammed into the wall, acquiring a new contusion to add to those already marring his head. "Where are you?" he panted, making grabs at the air. "You dirty, scheming, double-crossing, kidnapping, conniving snake-in-the-grass!"

"What are you getting so excited about?" the

voice yelped from the opposite corner. "What's Bever—I mean Lady Andragorre to you, you jailbird?"

"Jailbird, eh?" Lafeyette panted, stalking the detestable voice. "You're a swell one to talk, sitting here in your cell—" He jumped, almost got a grip on an arm, saw stars as a fist connected with his eye.

"Keep your distance, you!" the voice barked. "Troubles enough I didn't have, they had to toss a homicidal maniac in with me!"

"You lured her out of the city with your sweet talk, just so you could turn her over to her aunt! I mean to the old bat who was fronting for Krupkin!"

"That's what Rodolpho thought—but once I'd seen her, I had no intention of taking her there, of course—not that it's any of your business!"

"Where were you taking her? To some little love-nest of your own?"

"As a matter of fact, yes, big nose. And I'd have made it, too, if something hadn't set that gang of mounted police swarming through the woods. We had to run for it, and as luck would have it, that long-legged sheik, Lord Chauncy, was out hunting and nabbed us."

"Oh. Well, maybe it's just as well. At least here she has a decent bed."

"Oh? What do you know about Bever—I mean, Lady Andragorre's bed?"

"Plenty. I just spent an exciting half-hour under it."

"You did say—under it?"

"Exactly. I overheard her fending off the advances of that Chauncy character. I had my flying carpet—I mean my Mark IV personnel carrier—waiting right outside on the balcony. Just as I was about to whisk her away, the palace guard arrived."

"Yes, I warned Krupkin to keep an eye on Chauncy. Looks like they got there just in time, too!"

"Just too soon! I had her in my arms when they burst in on us—"

"Why, you—" An unseen body hurtled past O'Leary; he thrust out a foot and had the satisfaction of hooking an ankle solidly. The resultant crash went far to assuage the pain of his swelling eye.

"Listen, Lorenzo," Lafayette said, "there's no point in our flailing away at each other in the dark. Apparently we both have an interest in the welfare of Lady Andragorre. Neither of us wants to see her in Krupkin's clutches. Why don't we work together until she's safe and then settle our differences?"

"Work together, ha," Lafayette's unseen cellmate muttered from a point near the floor. "What's to work? We're penned in, empty-handed, in the dark. Unless," he went on, "you have something up your sleeve?"

"They cleaned me out," Lafayette said. "I had some dandy items: a two-way intercom sword, a blackout cloak, a fast-key, a flat-walker . . ." He paused, quickly felt for his belt. It was still in place. He unbuckled it, pulled it free, felt over the back, found the zipper tag there, pulled it.

"Hold everything, Lorenzo," he said tensely. "Maybe we're in business."

"What are you talking about?" the other came

back in his pettish voice. "Swords? Keys? What we need is a charge of dynamite, or a couple of stout crowbars."

"I may have something better," Lafayette said, extracting a flat two-inch by one-inch rectangle of what felt like flexible plastic from its hiding place under the zipper. "They missed the flat-walker."

"What's a flat-walker?"

"According to Pinchcraft, it generates a field which has the effect of modifying the spatial relationships of whatever it's tuned to, vis-á-vis the exocosm. It converts any one-linear dimension into the equivalent displacement along the perpendicular volumetric axis, at the same time setting up a harmonic which causes a reciprocal epicentric effect, and—"

"How would you go about explaining that to an ordinary mortal?" Lorenzo interrupted.

"Well, it reduces one of the user's physical dimensions to near zero, and compensates by a corresponding increase in the density of the matter field in the remaining quasi-two-dimensional state."

"Better try the idiot version."

"It makes you flat."

"How is wearing a corset going to help us?" Lorenzo yelped.

"I mean *really* flat! You can slide right between the molecules of ordinary matter—walk through walls, in other words. That's why it's called a flat-walker."

"Good grief, and I was practically outside, sneaking up on that long-legged son of a Schnauzer who pitched me in here."

"That's the spirit! Now stand fast, Lorenzo, and

I'll try this thing out. Let's see, Pinchcraft said to orient it with the long axis coinciding with my long axis, and the smooth face parallel to the widest plane of my body, or vice versa . . ."

"I suppose this was all part of their torture plan," Lorenzo muttered, "to lock me in with a mental case. I should have known better than to get my hopes up. Poor Beverly. With me put away, there's no one to help her. She'll hold out for as long as she can, but in the end the ceaseless importuning of her captor combined with the prospects of ruling this benighted principality will erode her will, and—"

"I read the same book," Lafayette said. "It was lousy. How about bottling up your pessimism while I conduct a test." Lafayette fingered the flat-walker, found the small bump at the center, and pressed it.

Nothing happened. He peered disappointedly into the surrounding blackness.

"Damn!" Lafayette said with feeling. "But I guess that would have been too easy. We'll have to think of something else. Listen, Lorenzo: how high is this room? Maybe there's a hatch in the ceiling, and if one of us stood on the other's shoulders, we could reach it." He stood on tiptoes and reached as far overhead as he could, but touched nothing. He jumped, still found no ceiling.

"How about it?" he snapped. "Do you want to climb up on my shoulders, or shall I get on yours?"

There was no answer. Even the mice had stopped rustling.

"Speak up, Lorenzo! Or have you gone back to

sleep?" He moved across toward the other's corner, feeling for the wall. After he had taken ten steps, he slowed, advancing cautiously. After five more steps, he halted.

"That's funny," he said in the circumambient darkness. "I thought the cell was only ten paces wide . . ."

He turned and retraced his steps, counting off fifteen paces, then went on another five, ten, fifteen steps. Abruptly, blinding light glared in his eyes. He blinked, squinting at what appeared to be a wall of featureless illumination, like the frosted glass over a light fixture. As he turned, the wall seemed to flow together; lines and flecks and blots of color appeared, coalesced into a normal though somewhat distorted scene: a dim-lit corridor, glass-walled, glass-floored, lined by heavy doors of black glass.

"I'm outside the cell!" he blurted. "It worked! Lorenzo—!" He turned, saw the walls expand as he did, stretching out into featurelessness, like a reflection in a convex mirror.

"Must be some effect of two dimensionality," he murmured. "Now, let's see—what direction did I come from?"

Squinting, he stepped hesitantly forward; the glare winked out to total darkness. He took fifteen paces and halted.

"Lorenzo," he hissed. "I made it!"

There was no answer.

"Oh—he probably can't hear me—or I can't hear him—with this gadget turned on . . ." Lafayette pressed the deactivating switch. There was no apparent change, except for the almost

imperceptible sounds of moving air—and a muffled sob.

"Oh, for heaven's sake, buck up," Lafayette
snapped. "Crying won't help!"

There was a startled intake of air.

"Lafe?" a familiar voice whispered. "Is it really
you?"

Lafayette sniffed garlic? "Swinehild!" he
gasped. "How did you get here?"

"Y-you told me not to follow you," Swinehild
was saying five minutes later, having enjoyed a
good cry while O'Leary patted her soothingly.
"But I watched the gate and seen you come
through. Happened there was a horse tied in front
of a beer joint, so I ups and takes off after you. The
feller on the ferry showed me which way you
went. When I caught up with you, you was smack
in the middle of a necktie party—"

"It was you that yowled like a panther!"

"It was all I could think of in a hurry."

"You saved my life, Swinehild!"

"Yeah. Well, I beat it out of there, and next thing
I knew I was lost. I spent some time wandering
around, and then my horse shied at something
and tossed me off in a berry bush. When I crawled
out of that, here was this old lady sitting on a
stump, lighting up a cigar. I was so glad to see a
human face, I waltzed right over and said how-do.
She jumped like she'd set on a cactus and give me
a look like I was somebody's ghost. 'Good Lord,'
she says. 'Incredible! But after all—why not?' I
was just starting to ask her if she'd seen the big
bird or whatever that'd spooked my critter, and

she outs with a tin can with a button on top and jams it in my face, and I get a whiff of mothballs, and that's all I know for a while."

"I believe I know the lady in question," Lafayette said grimly. "That's three scores I have to settle with her—if not more."

"After that I had some crazy dreams about flying through the air. I woke up in a nice room with a smooth-looking little buzzard that must of been the old dame's brother or something; they favored a lot. He asked me a lot of screwy questions, and I try to leave and he grabs me, and naturally, I swat him a couple and the next thing I know a strong-arm squad is bum's-rushing me down here." Swinehild sighed. "Maybe I shouldn't of been so fast with that right hook—but the slob had cold hands. But I should of known I didn't have to worry. I knew you'd find me, Lafe." Her lips nuzzled his ear.

"By the way," she whispered, "I brought the lunch. How about a nice hunk o' sausage and cheese? It's a little crumbly—I been carrying it tucked in my bodice—"

"No, thanks," Lafayette said hastily, disengaging himself. "We have to get out of here right away. I'm going to go back outside and find a key—"

"Hey, how'd you get in here Lafe? I never heard the door open . . ."

"I came through the wall. Nothing to it, just a trick I'll tell you about later. But I can't take you out that way. I'll have to get the door open. So if you'll just wait here—"

"You're going to leave me alone again?"

"It can't be helped, Swinehild. Just sit quietly

and wait. I'll be back as soon as possible. It shouldn't take too long."

"I . . . I guess you know best, Lafe. But hurry. I never did like being alone in the dark."

"Never fear, there's a good girl." He patted her shoulder. "Try to think about something nice, and I'll be back before you know it."

"G-g'bye, Lafe. Take care."

Lafayette groped his way to the wall, reactivated the flat-walker, waded forward into the glare of the corridor. Again he adjusted his eyes to the light and to the alternately stretched-out and compressed nature of visual phenomena. The narrow passage was still empty. He deactivated the flat-walker, saw the view slide into normality. He made his way stealthily along to the nearest cross-corridor. Two men in scarlet coats lounged in a lighted doorway twenty feet from the intersection. One of them, a paunchy, pasty-faced fellow with untrimmed hair, wore a large ring of keys dangling from his belt. There was no chance to approach them openly. Again O'Leary pressed the control switch of the flat-walker, saw the sides of the passage rush together while the solid glass walls beside him stretched out to a shimmering, opalescent blankness.

"Don't lose your bearings," he instructed himself sternly. "Straight ahead, about twenty paces; then rematerialize—and while they're catching their breath, grab the keys and go flat. Got it?

"Got it," he replied, and started forward.

At the first step, the lighted corridor shifted, collapsed, became a cloudy veil. Lafayette felt about him; nothing tangible met his hands.

"Must be some kind of orientation effect," he

suggested to himself. "Just keep going."

It was confusing, pushing forward into the milky glare. By turning his head sideways, O'Leary could see an alternate pattern of glass bricks which revolved away from him as he passed, like walking past an endless curved mirror. After five paces, he was dizzy. After ten, he halted and took deep breaths through his nose to combat the sensation of seasickness.

"Pinchcraft has a few bugs to iron out," he muttered, swallowing hard, "before the flatwalker is ready for the market." He forged on another five paces. How far had he come now? Ten paces? Or twenty? Or . . .

Something flashed and twinkled in front of him, surrounding him. There was a swirl of scarlet, a glitter of brass. Then he was staring directly into a set of what were unmistakably vertebrae, mere inches from his eyes, topped by a jellylike mass of pinkish material . . .

With a lunge, Lafayette leaped clear, gave a whinny of gratitude as darkness closed about him.

"Pinchcraft didn't warn me," he panted, "about walking through a man . . ."

It was a good five minutes before Lafayette felt equal to resuming his stalk. He picked a direction at random, took five more paces, two more for good measure, then halted and switched off the flat-walker.

"How'd you get out?" a surprised voice said as blazing sunlight flooded his retinas. Lafayette caught a swift impression of an open courtyard etched in light like a scene revealed by a flash of lightning, a grinning face under a feathered hat, a swinging billy-club—then the nearest tower fell on his head, and the world exploded into darkness.

Ten

"All I know is, yer Highness, the mug shows up in the exercise yard, blinking like a owl." The voice boomed and receded like surf on a tropical beach. "I ask him nice to come along, and he pulls a knife on me. Well, I plead wit' him to hand it over, no violence, like you said, and he tries a run fer it and slips on a banana peel and cracks hisself on the knob. So I lift him up real easy-like and bring him along, knowing yer Highness's interest in the bum, and frankly it beats me what all the excitement is about, after twenty-one years on the force—"

"Silence, you blithering idiot! I told you this subject was to receive kid-glove treatment! And you bring him to me with a knot on his skull the size of the royal seal! One more word and I'll have you thrown to the piranhas!"

Lafayette made an effort, groped for the floor, found it under his feet. He wrestled an eye open, discovered that he was standing, supported by a painful grip on his upper arms, in a large, high-ceilinged room adorned by tapestries, chandeliers, rugs, gilt mirrors, polished furniture of

169

rich, dark wood. In a comfortable-looking armchair before him sat a small, dapper man wearing a ferocious frown on his familiar, well-chiseled features.

"Go-go-go-go," Lafayette babbled, and paused for breath.

"Sergeant, if you've scrambled his wits, it's your head!" the gray-haired man yelped, rising and coming forward. "Lorenzo!" he addressed Lafayette. "Lorenzo, it's me, your friend, Prince Krupkin! Can you understand me?" He peered anxiously into O'Leary's face.

"I . . . I understand you," Lafayette managed. "But—but—you—you're—"

"Good lad! Here, you cretins, seat my guest here, on this pile of cushions. Bring wine! How's your head, my boy?"

"Terrible," Lafayette said, cringing at each pulsebeat. "I was almost over my hangover when I fell down the elevator, and I was almost over that when this lout clubbed me down. I must have three concussions running concurrently. I need a doctor. I need sleep. I need food. I need an aspirin—"

"You shall have it, dear lad. Along with my abject apologies for this dreadful misunderstanding. I hope you'll excuse my remarks at our last meeting, I was overwrought. I was just on the point of sending for you to make amends when the sergeant reported he'd encountered you wandering in the courtyard. Ah, by the way, how did you happen to be in the courtyard, if you don't mind my asking?"

"I walked through the wall—I think. It's all a little hazy now."

"Oh. To be sure. Well, don't worry about it, just relax, have a drink. A nap will fix you up nicely—just as soon as we've had a talk, that is."

"I don't want to talk, I want to sleep. I need an anesthetic. I probably need a blood transfusion, and possibly a kidney transplant. Actually I'm dying, so it's probably wasted effort—"

"Nonsense, Lorenzo! You'll soon be right as rain. Now, the point I wanted to inquire about—or about which I wanted to inquire, we must be grammatically correct, ha-ha—the point, I say, is—where is she?"

"Who?"

"Don't play the noddy, my lad," Prince Krupkin came back in a sharper tone. "You know whom."

"Tell me anyway."

Krupkin leaned forward. "The Lady Andragorre!" he snapped. "What have you done with her?"

"What makes you think I did anything with her?"

His Highness glared at O'Leary. He gripped his knuckles and cracked them with a sound that sent new waves of pain lancing through O'Leary's head.

"Who else would have had the audacity to spirit her away from the luxurious chambers in which I, from the goodness of my heart, installed the thankless creature?"

"Good question," O'Leary mumbled. "Lorenzo would be the likeliest suspect if he weren't in a cell . . ."

"Exactly! Which brings us back to the original query: where is she!"

"Beats me. But if she got away from you, good for her."

"I'll have the truth out of you if I have to extract it with red-hot pincers, you miserable ingrate!"

"I thought kid-glove treatment was the prescription," Lafayette said. His eyes were closed, watching the pattern of red blobs that pulsed in time with his heartbeat.

"I'll kid-glove you! I'll have the hide off your back under a cat-o'-nine-tails—" Krupkin broke off, took a deep breath, let it out between his teeth.

"Such are the burdens of empire," he muttered. "You try to give a vile wretch of a double-crossing sneak an even break, and what happens? He throws it in your face. . . ."

Lafayette forced both eyes open, looked long into the irate features of the prince.

"It's amazing," he muttered. "You talk just like him. If I hadn't already met Swinehild and Hulk and Lady Andragorre and Sprawnroyal, and Duke Rodolpho, I'd swear you were—"

"Ah, that slippery eel, Rodolpho! He seduced you from the path of duty, eh? What did he promise you? I'll double it! I'll triple it!"

"Well, let's see: as I recall, he said something about undying gratitude—"

"I'll give you ten times the gratitude that petty baron can bring to bear!"

"I wish you'd make up your mind," Lafayette said. "What's it to be, the red carpet or the rack?"

"Now, now, my boy, I was just having my little jest. We have great things to accomplish together, you and I! A whole world to whip into shape! The riches of all the mines and seas and forests, the fabled loot of the East!" Krupkin leaned forward, his eyes bright with plans. "Consider: no one here knows the location of the great diamond mines—the richest gold deposits—the rarest beds of emeralds! But you and I do—eh?" He winked. "We'll work together. With my genius for planning, and your special talents"—he winked again—"there's no limit to what we can accomplish!"

"Special talents? I play the harmonica a little—learned it via correspondence course—"

"Now, now, don't twit me, lad," Krupkin waggled a finger good-naturedly.

"Look, Krupkin—you're wasting your time. If the lady's not in her chambers, I don't know where she is." Lafayette held his head in his hands, supporting it delicately, like a cracked melon. Through his fingers he saw Krupkin open his mouth to speak, and suddenly freeze, lean forward, staring at him with an expression of total amazement.

"Of course!" the prince breathed. "Of course!"

"See something green?" Lafayette snapped.

"No. No, not at all. Not green at all. Amazing. That is to say, I don't notice a thing. I mean to say I didn't see anything at all. But it suddenly comes to me that you're tired, poor lad. Surely you'd like a hot tub and a few handmaidens to scrub your back, and a cozy bed to snuggle down in? And after you've rested, we can have a long chat about your further needs, eh? Splendid. Here!" The prince snapped his fingers at an attendant. "Prepare the imperial suite for my honored guest! A scented bath, my most exquisite personal masseuses—and let the royal surgeon attend with balms and unguents for this nobleman's hurts."

Lafayette yawned hugely. "Rest," he mumbled. "Sleep. Oh, yes . . ."

He was only half-aware of being led from the room, along a wide corridor, up a grand staircase. In a big, soft-carpeted chamber, gentle hands helped him out of his grimy garments, lowered him to a vast, foamy tub, scrubbed him, dried him, laid him away between crisp sheets. As the rosy light faded to sweet-scented gloom, he snuggled down with a sigh of utter contentment. . . .

Abruptly, his eyes were wide open, staring into the darkness.

"You and I know the location of the diamond mines . . . the gold deposits," he seemed to hear Krupkin's unctuous voice saying. *"With your special talents . . ."*

"Only someone from outside Melange— someone from a more highly developed parallel world—would know anything about gold mines and emerald beds," he muttered. "The geology is very much the same from world to world—and an outsider could dig into the Kimberley hills or the Sutter's Mill area and be dead sure of a strike. Which means Krupkin is an outsider—like me. And not only that—" Lafayette sat bolt upright. "He *knows* I'm an outsider! Which means he knew me before, which means he's who he looks like: Goruble, ex-king of Artesia! Which means he has a method of shifting from here to there, and maybe he can get me back to Artesia, and—"

Lafayette was out of bed, standing in the middle of the room. He groped, found a lamp, switched it on, went to the closet, extracted his clothes—

including the innocent-looking blackout cloak—neatly cleaned and pressed.

"But why is he interested in Lady Andragorre?" he ruminated as he dressed quickly. "And Swinehild? But—of course! Being who he is, he realizes that Swinehild is the double of Princess Adoranne, and that Lady Andragorre is Daphne's twin . . .

"Never mind that right now," he advised himself crisply. "Your first move is to get Daph—that is, Lady Andragorre—out of his clutches. And Swinehild too, of course. Then, when they're safely tucked away, you can talk from a position of strength, make some kind of deal to get home in return for not turning him into Central.

"Right," he agreed with himself. "Now, which way to the tower?" He went to the window, pulled aside the hangings, looked out at deep twilight, against which the minarets of the Glass Tree glittered like spires of varicolored ice. He visually traced the interconnecting walls and walkways and airy bridges linking the keep in which he found himself with the tall tower. "If I can just keep my sense of direction. . . ."

Silently he let himself from the room. A lone guard under a light at the far end of the passage failed to look around as he eased off along the deep-carpeted hall.

Three times in the next half-hour O'Leary reached a dead end, was forced to turn back and find another route. But at last he gained the circular stair down which the guards had dragged him some hours earlier, on the way to the dungeons.

On the landing above, he could see an armed guard in scarlet and white, yawning at his post. O'Leary went up silently, invisible inside his cloak, carefully cracked the man over the head, and laid him out on the floor. He tried the door. It was locked. He tapped.

"Lady Andragorre! Open up! I'm a friend! I came to help you escape!"

There was no answer, no sound from inside. He checked the guard, found a ring of keys, tried four before finding the correct one. The door swung in on a dark, untenanted room.

"Daphne?" he called softly. He checked the bathroom, the closet, the adjacent sitting room.

"It figures," he said. "Krupkin/Goruble said she was gone. But where could she have gotten to?"

He stepped out onto the balcony. The Mark IV was missing from the spot where he had left it propped against the wall. He groaned.

"Why didn't I hide it? But no, I was so loaded with gadgets and confidence, I thought I'd be back in ten minutes with Daphne, and off we'd go. So now I'm stuck—even if I found her, there'd be no way out." Lafayette left the room, closed the door behind him. The guard was just coming to, mumbling to himself. As Lafayette stepped over him, he caught the blurred words:

". . . not my fault, Sarge, I mean, how could anybody get loose outa a room at the top of a tower with only one way down, except if they jumped? And there ain't no remains in the courtyard down below, so my theory is the dame was never here in the first place . . ."

"Huh?" O'Leary said. "That's a good point. How could she have gotten away? Unless she took the Mark IV. But that's impossible. It's just an ordinary rug to anybody but me."

"Hey." The guard was sitting up, feeling of the back of his head. "I need a long furlough. First, I got these fainting spells, and now I hear voices . . ."

"Nonsense," O'Leary snapped. "You don't hear a thing."

"Oh. Well, that's a relief." The guard slumped back against the wall. "For a minute there I was worried."

"There's nothing I can do for Lady Andragorre now," Lafayette told himself, keeping his thought subvocal now. "But—good night, I've been forgetting all about Swinehild, poor kid, all alone down there in the dark. . . ." He hurried down the stairs, headed for the dungeons.

The passage was dark, narrow, twisting and turning its way downward to keep within the narrow confines of the spire of rock from which it had been hollowed. Lafayette passed barred doors behind which forlorn-looking prisoners in grimy rags and lengthening beards slumped dejectedly on straw bunks. The meager light came from unshielded fifteen-watt bulbs set in sockets at intervals along the way. The doors in the final, deepest section of the subterranean installation were solid slabs secured by heavy hasps and massive, rusted locks.

"The solitary-confinement wing," Lafayette murmured. "Close to paydirt now. Let's see . . . it must have been about here. . . ." He placed himself in the approximate spot at which he had emerged from the cell in which he had been confined with Lorenzo. As he studied the wall to orient himself—it wouldn't help to get the direction wrong again and wind up hanging in space, or back out in the courtyard—he heard stealthy footsteps approaching from around a curve above, down which he had just come. At once, he activated the flat-walker, waded forward into pitch darkness, switched back to natural density.

"Swinehild?" he called. "Swinehild?"

There was a soft clank and rasp of tumblers from behind him. A line of light appeared, widened. A male figure in a floppy hat with a broken, curling plume stood silhouetted there, holding a ring of keys in his hand.

"Lafayette!" an irritating voice hissed. "Are you here?"

"Lorenzo!" Lafayette said. "What are you doing here? I thought—"

"Well, so you did come back!" Lorenzo said in a relieved tone. "It's about time! This is the third time I've checked this pesthole! Let's go! This luck can't hold out forever!"

"I left you locked in; how did you get out?"

"Well—when I discovered you'd left without even saying good-bye, I knew there had to be a way—so I searched until I found the trapdoor in the ceiling. Since then I've had nothing but narrow escapes. Still, I suppose you were right about acting as if all this were real. At least it's more fun playing hide-and-seek around the palace with the guards than it was trying to sleep in here with the mice. Now, let's go—"

"Not without Lady A! She's disappeared—"

"I've got her. She's just outside the landing window, on your Mark IV. Nice little gadget, that.

Lucky this is just a dream, or I'd never have believed it when you described it. Now, let's get moving!"

"Swell," Lafayette grumbled. "It was supposed to be tuned to my personal wavelength . . ."

"Keep it quiet! The guards are playing pinochle at the head of the stairs."

"Wait a minute!" Lafayette called urgently. "Give me those keys. I have another detail to attend to—"

"Are you kidding? I risk everything on the off-chance you came back to the cell for me—out of a misguided feeling that I couldn't take your Mark IV and go off and leave you stranded—and you start babbling about errands you have to do!" He tossed the keys. "Do as you like; I'm on my way!"

Lafayette botched the catch. By the time he had retrieved the ring and jumped after Lorenzo, the latter was already disappearing around the tight curve of the passage.

"Hold the carpet for me!" O'Leary hissed. Hastily he examined the doors, picked one, tried keys. The door opened. From the darkness came a growl like a grizzly bear. O'Leary slammed it hurriedly, an instant before a heavy body struck the panel. He tried the next door—opened it a crack.

"Swinehild?" he called. This time he was rewarded by a quick intake of breath and a glad cry. There was a rustling near at hand, a faint whiff of garlic, and a warm, firm body hurled itself against O'Leary.

"Lafe—I figgered you'd went off without me!" Soft-skinned, hard-muscled arms encircled his neck. Eager lips found his.

"Mmmmhhhnnnmmm," O'Leary tried to

mumble, then discovered that the sensation of kissing Swinehild was not at all unpleasant—besides which, the poor girl's feelings would be hurt if he spurned her friendly advance, he reminded himself. He gave his attention to the matter for the next thirty seconds. . . .

"But looky here, Lafe, we can't get involved in no serious spooning now," Swinehild said breathlessly, coming up for air. "Let's blow outa this place pronto. It reminds me o' home. Here, you hold the lunch. It's rubbing a blister on my chest."

He stuffed the greasy parcel in his side pocket, took her hand, led her on tiptoe along the upward-slanting passage. Suddenly, from ahead, there was a sharp outbreak of voices: a deep, rasping challenge, a sharp yelp which sounded like Lorenzo, a feminine scream.

"Come on!" Lafayette broke into a run, dashed on ahead. The sounds of scuffling, gaps, blows grew rapidly louder. He skidded around the final turn to see two large men grappling with his former cellmate, while a third held the Lady Andragorre in a secure grip with one arm around her slender waist. At that moment one of the men kicked Lorenzo's feet from under him, threw him on his face, planted a foot on his back to hold him down. The man holding the girl saw O'Leary, goggled, opened his mouth—

Lafayette whipped the cloak around himself, took two quick steps forward, delivered a devastating punch to the solar plexus of the nearest guard, swung a hearty kick with his sharp-toed boot to the calf of the next. Dodging both victims' wild swings, he sprang to the Lady Andragorre's side and drove a knuckle blow to her captor's left kidney, grabbed her hand as the man yelled and released his grip.

"Don't be afraid! I'm on your side!" he hissed in her ear, and towed her quickly past the two whooping and cursing men. One made a grab at her, was rewarded with a clean chop across the side of the jaw that sent him to his knees with glazed eyes. Swinehild appeared, stared with wide-open eyes at Lady Andragorre, past O'Leary at something behind him.

"Lafe," she breathed. "Where'd you get that hat?"

"Quick! Get Lady Andragorre onto the rug outside the window at the next landing down," Lafayette barked, and thrust the girl forward.

"Gee, Lafe, I never knew you was a ventriloquist," Swinehild blurted as he turned back to see Lorenzo, just coming to all fours, his plumed cap awry, one eye black, a smear of blood under his nose. Lafayette hauled the dazed man to his feet, sent him staggering after the women.

"I'll hold these clowns off until you're aboard," he barked. "Make it fast!" He stepped forward to intercept one of the redcoats as he lunged after Lorenzo, tripped him, gave a side-handed chop to another, then whirled, raced down the passage after the others.

Swinehild's face was visible in the window ahead as she tugged at the still-dazed Lorenzo's hand.

"Who're you?" he said blurrily. "Aspira Fondell, the Music Hall Queen? Bu' I don' love you. I love Bev—I mean Lady Andragorre—or do I mean Beverly?"

"Sure, she's already aboard," Swinehild gasped. "Come on!" She hauled backward, and Lorenzo disappeared through the window with a wild leap. Muffled cries came from the darkness as Lafayette reached the open sash. Six feet away, the Mark IV carpet sagged in the air, sinking under the weight of the three figures huddled on it.

"She's overloaded." Swinehild's voice seemed thin and far away. "I guess we got one too many, Lafe—so—so I guess I won't be seeing you no more. Good-bye—and thanks for everything . . ." Before Lafayette's horrified gaze, she slipped over the side and dropped into the darkness below, while the carpet, quickly righting itself, slid away into the night.

"Oh, no!" Lafayette prayed. "She won't be killed—she'll land on a balcony just below here!" He thrust his head out the window. In the deep gloom he barely made out a slim figure clinging to a straggly bush growing from the solid rock fifteen feet below.

"Swinehild! Hang on!" He threw a leg over the sill, scrambled quickly down the uneven rock face, reached the girl, caught her wrist, tugged her upward to a narrow foothold beside him.

"You little idiot!" he panted. "Why in the world did you do that?"

"Lafe . . . you . . . you come back for me," she quavered, her pale face smiling wanly up at him. "But . . . but that means her Ladyship is all alone . . ."

"Lorenzo's with her, blast him," Lafayette reassured her, aware suddenly of his precarious position, of the cold wind whipping at him out of the surrounding night.

"Lorenzo? Who's he?"

"The clown in the floppy hat. He has some fantastic notion that the Lady Andragorre is his girl friend, some creature named Beverly. He's probably bound for that love-nest he was on his way to when Krupkin's men grabbed him."

"Gee, Lafe—I'm getting kind of mixed up. Things have been happening too fast for me. I guess I wasn't cut out for life in the big time."

"Me too," Lafayette said, looking up at the glassy wall above, then at the sheer drop below. He clutched his meager handholds tighter and squeezed his eyes shut.

"Which way do we go, Lafe?" Swinehild inquired. "Up or down?"

He tried a tentative move, slipped, grabbed, and clung, breathing shallowly so as not to disturb any boulders which might be delicately poised. The icy wind buffeted at him, whipped Swinehild's skirt against his legs.

"What we need," he said in a muffled voice, his face against the stone, "is a convenient door in the side of the mounain."

"How about that one over there?" Swinehild suggested as a tremor went through the rock under O'Leary.

"Where?" He moved his head cautiously, saw the small oak-plank door with heavy wrought-iron strap hinges set in a niche in the solid-rock wall ten feet to his left.

"We'll have to try," he gulped. "It's our only chance." He unclamped his aching fingers, edged a toe sideways, gained six inches. Five minutes of this painful progress gave him a grip on a tuft of weeds directly beside the door. He reached with infinite care, got his fingers on the latch.

"Hurry up, Lafe," Swinehild said calmly from behind him. "I'm slipping."

He tugged, lifted, pulled, twisted, pushed, rattled. The door was locked tight. He groaned.

"Why didn't I wish for an open door while I was at it?"

"Try knocking," Swinehild suggested in a strained voice.

Lafayette banged on the door with his fist, careless now of the pebbles dribbling away under his toe.

"No need to say good-bye again, I guess, Lafe," Swinehild said in a small voice. "I already done that. But it was sure nice knowing ya. You were the first fella that ever treated me like a lady . . ."

"Swinehild!" As her grip slipped, Lafayette lunged, caught her hand, clung. His own grip was crumbling—

There was a click and a creak from beside him; a draft of warm air flowed outward as the door swung in. A small, stocky figure stood there, hands on hips, frowning.

"Well, for Bloob's sake, come in!" Pinchcraft snapped. A calloused hand grabbed Lafayette, hauled him to safety; a moment later Swinehild tumbled in after him.

"H-h-how did you happen to be here?" O'Leary gasped, leaning against the chipped stone wall of the torchlit passage.

"I came with a crew to do a repossession." The Ajax tech chief bit the words off like hangnails.

"The idea was to sneak up and grab before he knew what hit him."

"Sure glad you did, Cutie-pie," Swinehild said.

"Don't call me Cutie-pie, girl," Pinchcraft barked. He took out a large bandanna and mopped his forehead, then blew his nose. "I told Gronsnart he was an idiot to keep on making deliveries on an arrears account. But no: too greedy for a quick profit, that's the business office for you."

"You're taking over the Glass Tree?"

"This white brontosaur? Not until the last hope of payment has faded. I was after the last consignment of portable goods we were so naïve as to deliver."

"Well, I'm glad you came. Look, we have to grab Krupkin at once! He's not what he seems! I mean, he *is* what he seems! He recognized me, you see—which means he's actually ex-King Goruble and not his double, but he doesn't know I know that, of course, so—"

"Calmly, sir, calmly!" Pinchcraft cut into the spate of words. "I was too late! The check-kiting fast-shuffler and his private army have flown the coop! He packed up bag and baggage and left here minutes before I arrived!"

Eleven

"Late again," Lafayette groaned. He was sitting, head in hands, at a table in the glittering, deserted dining room of the glass palace. A few servants and guards had eyed the party uncertainly as they invaded the building, but the sudden absence of their master combined with the rugged appearance of the repossession squad had discouraged interference. The well-equipped kitchens had been deserted by the cooks, but Swinehild had quickly rustled up ham and eggs and coffee. Now Pinchcraft's group sat around the table morosely, looking at the furniture and decor and mentally tallying up the probable loss on the job.

The Ajax representative said petulantly, "What about me? For the past three years this swindling confidence man who called himself Krupkin has been gathering resources—largely at the expense of Ajax—for some gradiose scheme. Now, abruptly, he decamps minutes before my arrival, abandoning all this!" Pinchcraft waved a hand to take in the installment-plan luxury all around them. "Now who's going to pay the bills?"

"Why did he suddenly abandon his plans?"

Lafayette inquired. "Could he have been afraid of me—afraid I'd tip Central off to his takeover bid?"

Pinchcraft was frowning in deep puzzlement. "Are you saying, lad, that you know about Central? But that's—that's the second most closely guarded secret of the Ajax Specialty Works!"

"Sure—I'm a sort of parttime Central agent myself," Lafayette said. "But Goruble knew me; and that must be why he packed up and left in the middle of the night—after first bundling me off to bed to get me out of the way. He was afraid I'd recognize him; but I was so dopey with lack of sleep I didn't know what I was doing. By the time I realized—it was too late." He sat down heavily and groaned again. "If I'd just gone straight to his apartment, instead of wasting time trying to find Lady Andragorre, I'd be back home by now."

"Don't take it too hard, Lafe," Swinehild said. "You done your best."

"Not yet, I haven't!" Lafayette smacked a fist into his palm. "Maybe I can still get ahead of him. He doesn't know I know what I know—not that I know much. But I still have an ace or two: Goruble doesn't know I know who and what he is. And he doesn't know I have a line of credit with Ajax!"

"Who says you have a line of credit with Ajax?" Pinchcraft cut in.

"Well—under the circumstances—since you and I are interested in the same thing: laying Krupkin/Goruble by the heels . . ."

"Well—all right," Pinchcraft muttered. "Within limits. What do you have in mind?"

"I need to get back to Port Miasma and tip Rodolpho off. Maybe between us we can throw a stillson wrench into Goruble's plans. How about it, Pinchcraft? Will you help me?"

"I suppose it can be arranged—but you already owe us for a number of items—"

"We'll settle all that later. Let's get moving; it's a long walk, and time's of the essence and all that."

"I suppose I can crowd you into the tunnel car we came in," Pinchcraft said reluctantly. "Even though it's supposed to be for official use only."

"Tunnel car? You mean there's a tunnel all the way from here to the Ajax plant?"

"Certainly. I told you I never trusted this fellow—"

"Then why," Lafayette demanded, "was I sent out here on that flimsy little Mark IV carpet? I could have broken my neck!"

"All's well that end's well," Pinchcraft pointed out. "I needed a diversion to cover my repossession. And when would I ever have a better chance to field-test the equipment? Let's go, men. The night's work's not over yet!"

It was a fast, noisy, dusty ride in a child-sized subway train that hurtled along the tracks laid through the twisting series of caverns underlying the miles of desert over which O'Leary had flitted so nervously the previous night. Swinehild cuddled next to him in the cramped seat and slept soundly until the car docked at their destination. She oohed and ahed at the sights as they left the terminus and made their way through vast workshops, foundries, stamping plants, refineries, the odors and tumult of a busy underground manufacturing operation.

"I've always heard about elves toiling away

under the mountain," Lafayette confided in his
guide as they emerged into the comparative quiet
of the admin level. "But I always pictured little
fellows with beards pounding out gold arm rings
at a hand forge."

"We modernized a while back," Sprawnroyal
told him. "Production's up eight hundred percent
in the last fiscal century alone."

In the retail-sales department, Swinehild
watched in silence as a bustling crew of electronics men rolled out a small, dark-green carpet
at Pinchcraft's instruction.

"This is our Mark XII, the latest model," the
production chief stated proudly. "Windscreen,
air and music, safety belt, and hand-loomed deep
pile as soft as goofer feathers."

"It's cute," Swinehild said. "But where do I
sit?"

"You can't go," O'Leary said shortly. "Too
dangerous."

"I am too going," she came back sharply. "Just
try and stop me!"

"You think I'd risk your neck on this contraption? Out of the question!"

"You think I'm going to sit around this marble
factory ducking my head under the ceiling while
you go off and get yourself killed?"

"Not on your life, lady," Sprawnroyal said.
"Fitzbloomer, roll out a Mark XIII—a two-seater."
He gave O'Leary a challenging look. "Anybody
thinks I'm going to get myself saddled with the
care and feeding of a broad two feet higher'n me's
got wrong ideas."

"Well . . . in that case," O'Leary subsided.

It was the work of ten minutes to check circuits,

carry the Mark XIII to a launching platform on the face of the cliff, and balance out the lift system for a smooth, level ride.

"Contraption, eh?" Pinchcraft snorted under his breath. "She'll handle like an ocean liner. Just hold her under sixty for the first few miles, until you get the feel of her."

"Sure," Lafayette said, tucking his fur-lined blackout cloak around him against the bitter night wind. Swinehild settled herself behind him, with her arms around his waist.

"Here we go," O'Leary said. There was the familiar lifting surge, a vertiginous moment as the rug oriented itself on the correct course line. Then the wind was whistling past their faces as the lights of the Ajax Specialty Works receded behind them.

"I hope you ain't mad at me for coming along," Swinehild whispered in Lafayette's rapidly numbing ear.

"No, not really," O'Leary called over his shoulder. "Just don't get in my way when the action starts to hot up. Krupkin beat it because he was afraid I'd realize who he was and unleash my psychic energies on him." He gave a humorless chuckle. "I recognized him, all right—but what he doesn't know is that I haven't got a psychic erg to my name anymore."

"You've got luck," Swinehild pointed out. "Like finding that door into the tunnel just when you did. That's just about as good, I guess."

"There's something strange about my luck," O'Leary said. "It's either unbelievably bad, or unbelievably good. Like finding that disguise in the park—and before that, in the boat, coming up with a knife just when I need it: sometimes it's almost as if my psychic energies were back at work. But then I try again, and draw a goose egg. It's very unsettling."

"Don't worry bout it, Lafe. Just take it as it comes. That's what I do—and somehow I always get by."

"That's all very well foryou," O'Leary countered. "All you're interested in is getting to the big town and living high; as for me—there are times when I almost wish I was still back at Mrs. MacGlint's, with nothing to worry about but earning enough to keep me in sardines and taffy."

"Yeah—you got it rough, all right, Lafe, being a hero and everything."

"Hero? Me?" O'Leary laughed modestly. "Oh, I'm not really a hero," he assured his companion. "I mean, heroes love danger: they're always dashing around looking for adventure, and that sort of thing. Whereas all I want is peace and quiet."

"You could have peace and quiet easy enough, Lafe. Just turn this rug around and head for the south. I hear there's some nice islands down that way where we could build us a grass hut and live on coconuts and fresh fish—"

"Would that I could, Swinehild. But it's not that easy. First I have to deal with Krupkin/Goruble, the skunk! I just wish I could get my hands on him right now! I'd like to see the look on his face when I tell him I know who he is and what he's up to, and—"

The rug bumped, as if hitting an updraft.

"Look out!" Swinehild cried as something white loomed directly before them. Lafayette yelled a command to the Mark XIII—too late. The carpet banked sharply to the left, struck, plowed through a drift of snow as fine as confectioner's sugar, upended, and went cartwheeling downslope in a cloud of ice crysals. Lafayette was aware of Swinehild's arms clinging to him, of the safety belt cutting into his ribs, of flying snow slashing at him like a sand blaster. . . .

With a final sickening drop, the rug came to rest half-buried in loose ice. Lafayette struggled upright, saw moving lights, blurred figures, heard gruff voices, the stamp of hooves. . . .

"It's *you*," a familiar voice blurted. "How—what—when—but most of all, *why*? I left you snoozing soundly in sybaritic luxury. What are you doing out here in the snow?"

O'Leary blinked away the slush from his eyelashes, gazed blearily up at the anxious visage of Goruble/Krupkin. Behind him, uniformed men stood gaping.

"Thought you'd steal a march, eh?" Lafayette said brokenly. "Well, you won't get away with it, your Former Majesty. I know you—and I know what you're planning . . ." He tugged at the rug, which had somehow wrapped itself around him, but he was bound as tightly as if by ropes.

"S-see here, my boy," Goruble stammered, waving his men back. "Can't we work something out? I mean, you have your cushy spot, why begrudge me mine? It's not easy, you know, having been a king, to revert to mere commonerhood. Why not take the charitable view? With your help, I can be back on the Artesian throne in a lightning coup, after which you'll have your pick of the spoils—or better yet, I'll give you all of Melange, to do with as you will—"

"Forget it," O'Leary said, surreptitiously striving to free an arm. "I have everything I want, back in Artesia. Why would I want to help you?"

"But here you can be absolute owner of everything—the real estate, wildlife, natural resources . . . women . . ."

"Stay in Melange? Are you crazy? I can't wait to get home. I've had nothing but misery since I got here!"

Goruble opened his mouth to speak, hesitated, looked suddenly thoughtful.

"In that case," he asked carefully, "why haven't you done something about it?"

"Well—"

"You were, as I recall, in rather difficult straits when my chaps first apprehended you. And now—well, from the mode of your arrival, it appears that you are perhaps somewhat less than master of your fate." The ex-king rubbed his chin. "You are Lafayette O'Leary—I saw your ring. Only you wear the ax and dragon. But . . . can it be, dear lad"—his voice took on a purr like a tiger about to dine—"that you have in some way lost your valuable ability to manipulate the probabilities at will? Eh?"

"Of course not. I . . . I was just wishing I could have a chat with you, and . . . and here I am."

"Yes—with a mouthful of snow and a number of new contusions that are already beginning to swell, no doubt. Very well, Sir Lafayette: before we discuss matters further, just demonstrate your puissance by, oh, summoning up a cozy little tent, say, complete with camp stove and liquor cabinet, in which we can complete our negotiation."

"Phooey," Lafayette said weakly. "I wouldn't waste my time."

"Something simpler, then: what about a small, cheery blaze in the shelter of the rocks, there. . . ." Goruble waved a hand at the curtain of falling snow.

"Why bother?" O'Leary gulped. "Why don't you just surrender, and I'll put in a good word for you with Mr. Pratwick . . ."

"Admit it!" Goruble leaned close to hiss the words. "You're impotent to interfere! You're as helpless as the clod you appear to be!"

"I am not," Lafayette said desperately. "I have all kinds of resources at my disposal!"

"Then let's see you get yourself extricated from that piece of rug you seem to be ensnarled in."

Lafayette pulled, twisted, wrenched; but it was no use. He was wrapped as tightly as a caterpillar in a cocoon. Goruble laughed happily.

"Capital! Oh, capital! I've had a nervous night for nothing! I don't know how it is you happen to have stumbled on my little base of operations here, Sir Lafayette, but there's no harm done after all. In fact . . ." He sobered suddenly, nodding. "I can see that a whole new dimension might be added to my plans, so to speak. Yes, why not? With the new data this development places at my disposal, why stop with Melange? Why not move on—expand my empire to encompass a whole matched set of worlds, eh? In the meantime— where's the elusive doxy you stole from me?"

"Where you'll never find her," Lafayette said.

"Reticent eh? Well, we'll soon correct that. Oh, we'll have long talks, my lad. My liegeman, Duke

Rodolpho, retains a skilled interrogator in his employ, one Groanwelt by name, who'll soon wring your secrets from you!" Goruble whirled, bawled orders; red-coated men with ice in their eyelashes leaped forward to lift Lafayette to his feet, peel the frozen rug away—

"Hey—a dame!" a man blurted as Swinehild appeared from the folds of the Mark XIII, dazed and shivering.

Goruble laughed merrily. "My luck has turned at last!" he cried. "The fates smile on my enterprise! I take this as a sign—a sign, do you hear?" He looked on, beaming as the grinning men pulled the girl to her feet, keeping a stout grip on her arms. For the moment, the carpet lay in an unattended heap. Lafayette made a sudden lunge for it, but was quickly grabbed, but with a final surge, he managed to plant a foot on the snow-covered nap.

"Go home!" He addressed the yell to the receiver's verbal input circuitory. "Top speed and no detours!"

In response the carpet flopped, sending up a spray of ice crystals, leaped six feet into the air, hung for a moment rippling, then, as one of the men made a belated grab, shot away into the gathering storm.

" 'Tis enchanted, by crikey!" a man yelled, recoiling.

"Nonsense," Goruble snapped. "It's undoubtedly another gadget from Ajax. So you're working with those sharpies, eh, Sir Lafayette? But no matter: I have my plans for them, as well as the rest of this benighted land!"

"You've sprung your seams," Lafayette

snapped. "Your last takeover bid flopped, and so will this one."

"Truss them and hoist them on horseback," Goruble commanded the captain of his guard. "We'll see what a night in the cold followed by a day on the rack does for this upstart's manners."

"Well, back again, hey, pal?" Rodolpho's physical-persuasion specialist greeted O'Leary cheerfully as four guards dumped him, more dead than alive, on a wooden bench near the fireplace in which half a dozen sets of tongs and pincers were glowing a cozy cherry red.

"Mnnnrrgghhh," O'Leary mumbled through stiff lips, crouching nearer the blaze. "Just give me heat, even if it's my own feet burning."

"Anything to oblige, chum. Now, lessee, where were we?" Groanwelt rubbed a hand over his bristled chin with a sound like tearing canvas. "We could start out wit' a little iron work, like you suggested, then move on to a few strokes o' the cat, just to get the old circulation going good, and wind up the session wit' a good stretch on the rack to take the kinks out. How's it sound?"

"A well-balanced program, no doubt," Lafayette mumbled. "Could you stoke up this fire a little first?"

"That's the spirit, kid. Say, on the other hand, maybe you'd like to try the new equipment I just got in since you was here: a swell hydraulic-type joint press, roller bearings throughout. A versatile outfit: handles everything from hip sockets to knuckles. But maybe we better save that and the automatic skinning machine for last; they're kind of permanent, if you know what I mean. We don't

want you graduating on us before we get the dope,
which the duke wants it pretty bad."

"It's not the duke, it's that sneaky little Krupkin
who thinks I'm going to spill a lot of secrets,"
Lafayette corrected the P.P.S. "Listen, Groanwelt,
as a loyal Melanger, you should be fighting Krupkin, not helping him. His scheme is to take over
the whole country and use it as a base of operations to launch an attack on Artesia!"

"Politics," Groanwelt said apologetically, "was
never a big hobby wit' me. I mean, administra-
tions come and go, but the need for a skilled
specialist remains constant—"

"Don't you have any patriotism?" O'Leary chal-
lenged. "This man's a maniac! He'll loot Melange
of everything useful: food, weapons, raw
materials—and—"

"Sure, fella. But look, OK if we get started?
You can talk while I work. How's about getting
the shirt off and stepping over here so's I can
buckle you up in working position?"

"C-couldn't I just toast my toes for a few minutes longer?"

"Good notion. I'll help you off wit' the boots,
and we'll strap the ankles up nice to hold 'em in
optimum position. Too close, and you get a lot o'
smoke; too far, and you don't get the full effect,
like—"

"On second thought, why don't I tell you whatever you want to know right now, and save you all
that effort?" O'Leary suggested hurriedly.
"Where shall I start? With my arrival on top of the
windmill, two weeks ago? Or was it three? Or
should I go farther back, to when I had everything
in the world any sane man could want, and it

wasn't enough? Or—"

"Hey, hey, hold on, pal!" Groanwelt lowered his voice, looking around nervously. "What you trying to do, put me out o' business?"

"Not at all, but it just happens I'm in a talkative mood this evening—"

"It's morning. Geeze, kid, you're out o' touch."

"Yes, morning, evening, it doesn't matter, I love to talk night and day. Now, as I was saying—"

"Shhhh!" The P.P.S. laid a thick finger across his poonched-out lips. "Have a heart! You want to lose me the best post on the ducal staff? You go blowing your gaff wit'out me even laying a iron to you, and somebody's going to start getting ideas about redundant personnel. At my age, I can't take no RIF, kid. So be a sweet guy and button it up, hah?"

"I . . . I'll tell you what," Lafayette proposed, eyeing the smoking forceps in the technician's hairy fist. "You hold off with the irons for a few minutes—just until I do a few yoga exercises to heighten my appreciation of your virtuosity—and I'll try to bottle up the speech I want to make."

"Say, that's white o' you, neighbor!"

"Think nothing of it, Groanwelt. Glad to be helpful. By the way, do you have any idea what became of the young lady who arrived when I did?"

"Oh, her? Yeah. Say, cleaned up, she wouldn't be a bad-looking little piece, you know? I think I seen the boys handing her over to the house-keeper. Seems like your pal Prince Krupkin's got some kind o' special plans for her." Groanwelt winked.

"The rat," Lafayette snarled between his teeth.

"Groanwelt, you seem like a decent sort of chap: are you going to sit quietly by while that unprincipled crook carries out his plans right over your head, without a word?"

The P.P.S. sighed. "Yeah, I know, the idealism o' yout'. You young guys think you can cure the world o' its ills. But as you get a little older, you find out it ain't so easy. Me, I've settled for the pride o' craftsmanship: the integrity o' the skilled technician. I give every job the best that's in me, no shoddy work to have to be ashamed of later. I mean, when people are looking at a project o' mine, I want to be able to hold my head up, right? Speaking o' which, maybe we better start in; old Rodolpho's likely to show up any minute to check on progress—"

"He just did," a cold voice spoke up. The P.P.S. whirled to see Duke Rodolpho glowering at him from the doorway.

"Geeze!" he exclaimed. "I sure wish you wouldn't come pussyfooting up on a guy that way, y'er Grace! You give me such a start, I ain't sure I can go on wit' my work." He held up his hands, studying them for tremors.

"Never mind that," Rodolpho snapped. "You're about to be honored by a visit from his Highness. Now tighten up here and try to make a good impression . . ." The duke turned as bustlings sounded from the corridor behind him.

"Ah, right this way, my dear prince," he said through a forced smile. "A modest installation, but fully equipped—"

"Yes, yes, I'm sure," Krupkin cut him off, sauntering into view attended by a pair of lackeys who seemed to be trying to shine his shoes at full gallop. His sharp eyes swept the chamber, fell on Lafayette. He grunted.

"Leave us, Rudy," he ordered offhandedly. "And take these pests with you," he added, kicking at the fellow attempting to adjust the hang of his robes. "You stay," he addressed Groanwelt.

"But I haven't had a chance to show you the newly equipped forcing vats yet—" Rodolpho protested.

"You have our leave to withdraw!" Krupkin/Goruble barked. As the rest of the party hastily evacuated the room, the prince came over to O'Leary, who rose to face him. The ex-king looked him up and down, glanced at the ring on his finger. He hooked his thumbs in the broad, bejeweled belt encircling his middle and thrust out his lower lip

"All right, Sir Lafayette," he said in a tone inaudible to the P.P.S., who hovered uncomfortably in the background, polishing an iron boot. "Last chance. Your value to me, minus your former abilities, is small, but still, your cooperation might smooth my path a trifle. I've spent the last few hours reviewing my plans, and have realized that I've been thinking too small. Conquer Melange, indeed! As you pointed out, the place is a pesthole. But new vistas have opened themselves. Your presence here shows me the way. It was your meddling that lost me my throne in Artesia. Now you'll help me recover it."

"Don't talk like a boob," O'Leary said tiredly. "After what you tried to do to Adoranne, the people would throw stones at you if you ever showed your face in Artesia, even if you could get back there, which I doubt."

Goruble poked O'Leary's chest. "Cast aside your doubts, Sir Lafayette! That part is simplicity itself. Less than an hour ago I dispatched a set of specifications to our mutual friends of the Ajax Specialty Works, and expect delivery of a functioning Traveler in a matter of days."

"You're going to be disappointed. Your credit's shot. They won't deliver."

"Indeed?" Goruble/Krupkin purred, fingering a large jewel pinned to his collar. "I have reason to expect the early acquisition of new resources, courtesy of my good friend Duke Rodolpho. As for the possible animosity of the Artesians—I feel sure it will dissipate as the morning mist before a public declaration by Princess Adoranne that the previous canards spread regarding me were a tissue of lies homologated by enemies of the state; that I am in fact her sole benefactor, and that she wishes to relinquish the crown to me as an older and wiser monarch, solely out of her selfless concern for the well-being of the state."

"She'll never do it," O'Leary declared flatly.

"Perhaps not," Goruble said clamly, nodding. He poked O'Leary again, as one imparting the punch line of a joke. "But the wench Swinehild will."

"What's Swinehild got to do with it . . ." O'Leary's voice trailed off. "You mean—you intend to try to use her to impersonate Adoranne?" He smiled pityingly. "Wise up, Goruble; Swinehild's a nice kid, but she'd never fool anyone."

Goruble turned, barked an order at Groanwelt. The P.P.S. went to the door, thrust his head out, passed on the command. There was a stir of feet. Groanwelt stepped back, gaping, then executed a sweeping bow as a slim, dainty figure entered the room hesitantly. Lafayette stared openmouthed at the vision of feminine enchantment who stood there, gowned, jeweled, perfumed, elegant, her golden hair a gleaming aura about her perfect face.

"P-Princess Adoranne!" he gulped. "Wha— how—"

"Lafe! Are you O.K., sugar?" Swinehild's familiar voice inquired worriedly.

"I confess we need to do a little work in her diction before she makes her public appearance," Goruble said blandly. "But that's a mere detail."

"Swinehild—you wouldn't help this fiend with his dirty schemes—would you?" O'Leary implored.

"He . . . he said if I didn't—he'd slice you up into sandwich meat, Lafe—so—"

"Enough! Take her away!" Goruble roared, red-faced. He whirled on O'Leary as Groanwelt bowed Swinehild out.

"The doxy is merely attempting to save face," he snarled. "She leaped at the chance to play princess, as well she might, kitchen slavey that she is! To sleep on silken sheets, dine from dishes of gold—"

"And what about the real Adoranne?"

"There appears to be a certain symmetry in these matters of intercontinual transfer," Goruble said with a foxy smile. "The former princess will find herself here in Melange in the role of scullery wench, a fitting comeuppance in return for her arrogant assumption of my throne." Goruble rubbed his hands together. "Yes, you opened new vistas, lad, once I realized you were who you are.

My original plan in decoying the Lady Andragorre into my hands was designed merely to place me in an advantageous position, trump-wise, vis-à-vis Rodolpho, who'd been recalcitrant in seeing the wisdom of my plans. But now wide vistas open. She'll be a useful pawn in the vast new game I'll play, as will the feckless Rodolpho, lending their countenances to my pronouncements. And you, too, have your little role to perform." His face hardened. "Assist me—willingly—and you'll retain your comfortable Artesian sinecure as palace hanger-on. Refuse, and I'll arrange a fate for you to make strong men shudder!"

"You've lost what wits you ever had if you think I'd help you with your miserable plot!"

"So? A pity. I had in mind that after their usefulness to me had ended, I might hand the females along to you to use as you will. But in your absence, alas, I fear they'll end up in the harem of some more devoted servant."

"You wouldn't!"

"Oh, but I would." Goruble wagged a finger. "That's the true secret of success, my boy: total ruthlessness. I've learned my lesson now. Had I disposed of the infant Princess Adoranne in the beginning—and of a certain infant Prince Lafayette as well—none of this unfortunate business would have occurred."

"I won't help you," Lafayette gulped. "Do your worst. Central will catch up with you and—"

Goruble laughed. "That's the true beauty of the plan, my dear boy! I admit that for long the threat of Central's meddling inhibited the free play of my imagination—but the new equation of power renders that prospect nugatory. The reciprocal transfer of personnel will maintain the net energy equations; there will be no imbalance in the probability matrix, nothing to attract Central's attention to peaceful Artesia, one locus among a myriad. No, look for no assistance from that direction. As a former inspector of continua, please be assured that I know whereof I speak. Now, be sensible: throw in with me, and share in the rewards of success."

"Go hang yourself," O'Leary suggested sharply. "Without me, Swinehild will never cooperate—and without her, the whole thing flops."

"As you will." Goruble smiled a crafty smile. "My offer to you was based on sentiment, my lad, nothing more. I have more than one string to my bow—or should I say more than one beau to my string?"

"You're bluffing," Lafayette said. "You talk about using Lady Andragorre to impersonate Daphne—but I happen to know she got away clean!"

"Did she?" Goruble yawned comfortably, turned to Groanwelt. "By the way, my man," he said. "It won't be necessary to extract the whereabouts of the Lady Andragorre from this treacher. She and her companion were nabbed half an hour ago, and will be arriving within minutes. Just throw him in the pit with Gorog the Voracious, who I'm informed hasn't been fed for several days, and will appreciate a good meal."

"The breaks of the game, buddy," Groanwelt said sorrowfully as he led Lafayette, chains clanking, along the dim passage. "I got enemies around this place, that's plain to see. Me, a inoffensive guy that never stepped on a toe in his life except in line o'duty. But that goes to show you what years o' faithful service do for a guy." He peered through the inch-thick bars of a vast, barred door. "Good; he's in his den, sleeping. I won't have to use the electric prod to keep him back while I slip you in. I hate to be cruel to dumb beasts, you know?"

"Listen, Groanwelt," Lafayette said hastily, recoiling from the dank odor and the bone-littered straw of the monster's cage. "In view of our long-standing relationship, couldn't you see your way clear to just slip me out the back way? I mean, the duke need never know—"

"And leave Gorog miss another meal? I'm ashamed o' you, pal. The suggestion does youse no credit."

The P.P.S. unlocked the door, swung it open just far enough to admit O'Leary, whom he helped forward with a hand like a winepress clamped to his shoulder. Lafayette dug in his heels, but Groanwelt's thrust propelled him into the noisome cage and the door clanged behind him.

"So long, kid," the P.P.S. said, resecuring the lock. "You would of been a swell client. Too bad I never really got to the nitty wit' you." As his footsteps died away, a low, rumbling growl sounded from the dark opening cut in the side wall of the den. Lafayette whirled to face the mouth of the lair, a ragged arch wide enough to pass a full-grown tiger. A pair of bleary, reddish eyes glinted from the deep gloom there. A head thrust forth—not the fanged visage of a cat or a bear, but a low-browed, tangle-haired subhuman face, smeared with dirt and matted with black stubble. The low, rumbling growl sounded again.

"Excuse me," a hoarse, bass voice said. "I ain't eaten in so long my insides is starting to chew on theirselfs."

O'Leary backed. The head advanced, followed by massive shoulders, a barrellike torso. The huge creature stood, dusted off its knees, eyeing Lafayette speculatively.

"Hey," the deep voice rumbled. "I know you! You're the guy was with the cute little trick that laid me out with a oar!"

"Crunch!" Lafayette gasped. "How—how did you get here? I thought this was the den of Gorog the Voracious . . ."

"Yeah, that's the name I usta fight under. The duke's boys picked me up on a bum rap when I come looking for ya. I cleaned up a couple blocks o' city street with the slobs, but after a while I got tired and they felled me with a sneak attack from bot' flanks at oncet, plus they dropped a cannon-ball on my dome." The giant fingered the back of his massive skull tenderly.

"L-looking for me?" O'Leary was backed against the wall; his breath seemed to be con-stricted by a bowling ball that had dropped into his throat. "W-whatever for?"

"I got a little score to settle with you, chum. And I ain't a guy to leave no unfinished business laying around."

"Look here, Crunch, I'm the sole support of twin maiden aunts," O'Leary stated in a voice with a regrettable tendency to break into a falset-to. "And after all I've been through, it wouldn't be fair for it all to end here, like this!"

"End? Heck, bub, this is just the beginning," Crunch growled. "A score like I got with you'll take a while to pay off."

"What did I do to deserve this?" O'Leary groaned.

"It ain't what you done, sport, it's what you didn't do."

"Didn't do?"

"Yeah. You didn't put me over the side o' the boat when you had the chanct. I was groggy but still listening; I heard the little dolly make the suggestion, which you nixed it on account of you didn't think it was cricket to toss a unconscious guy to the sharks."

"So this is my r-reward?"

"Right, palsy." The giant put a hand to his midriff as his stomach emitted another volcanic growl. "Boy, I ain't had a good feed in a bear's age."

Lafayette squeezed his eyes shut. "All right," he gasped. "Hurry up and get it over with before I lose my nerve and start yelling to Groanwelt that I've changed my mind . . ."

"Get what over with, feller?"

"E-eating me." Lafayette managed to force the words out.

"Me—eat you?" Crunch echoed. "Hey, you got me wrong, pal. I wouldn't eat no guy which he saved my neck like you done."

O'Leary opened one eye. "You mean—you're not going to tear me limb from limb?"

"Why would I wanta do a thing like that?"

"Never mind," Lafayette said, sinking down to

the floor with a deep sigh of relief. "Some subjects are better left uninvestigated." He drew a deep breath and pulled himself together, looked up at the tall figure peering down at him concernedly.

"Look—if you want to do me a favor, let's start by figuring out a way to get out of here."

Crunch scratched at his scalp with a forefinger the size of a hammer handle.

"Well, lessee . . ."

"We might try to tunnel through the wall," O'Leary said, poking at the mortar between the massive stone blocks. "But that would take steel tools and several years." He scanned the dark interior of the cell. "There might be a trapdoor in the ceiling . . ."

Crunch shook his head. "I been ducking under that ceiling for a week. It's solid oak, four inches thick."

"Well . . . maybe the floor . . ."

"Solid rock, six inches thick."

Lafayette spent ten minutes examining floor, walls, and door. He leaned disconsolately against the bars. "I may as well admit it," he said. "I'm licked. Krupkin will force Swinehild to do his bidding, Adoranne will wind up scraping grease off pots here in Port Miasma, Goruble will take over Artesia, and Daphne—Daphne will probably be dumped here when Lady Andragorre goes to Artesia, and if Rodolpho doesn't get her, Lorenzo the Lucky—or is it Lancelot the Lanky?—will."

"Hey—I got a idear," Crunch said.

"Just lie down and take a nap, Crunch," O'Leary said listlessly. "There's nothing else to do."

"Yeah, but—"

"It's just self-torture to go on thinking about it. Maybe the best bet would be for you to disassemble me after all."

"Hey, how's about if—"

"I should have known it would end up here. After all, I've been bouncing in and out of jails ever since I got to Melange; it was inevitable that I'd end in one eventually."

"I mean, it ain't a fancy scheme, but what the heck," Crunch said.

"What scheme?" O'Leary inquired dully.

"What I was trying to tell you. My plan."

"All right. Tell me."

"Well, what I was thinking—but naw, I guess you want something with a little more class—like with secret tunnels and all."

"You may as well get it off your chest, Crunch."

"Well—I'm just spitballing, mind youse—but, ah, how's about if I rip the door off its hinges?"

"If you ri—" Lafayette turned to gaze at the massive welded-steel construction. He laughed hollowly.

"Sure, go ahead."

"O.K." Crunch stepped past him, gripped the thick bars. He set his size seventeens, took a deep breath, and heaved. There was a tentative screech of metal, followed by sharp snapping sounds. A lump of stone popped from the wall and dropped to the floor. With a rending sound comparable to that which might be produced by two Rolls-Royces sideswiping each other, the grating buckled, bent inward, and tore free of its mountings. Crunch tossed it aside with a deafening crash and wiped his palms on the seat of his leather pants.

"Nothing to it, chum," he said. "What's next?"

There was no one in the torture chamber when Lafayette, freed of his manacles by a deft twist of Crunch's wrists, and his large companion made their way there along the torchlit passage, past cells through the barred doors of which wild-haired and wild-eyed inmates gaped, gibbered, or grabbed.

"That's bad," Lafayette said. "I was counting on Groanwelt helping us."

"Hey, this is kinda cute," Crunch said, hefting a set of razor-edged cutters designed for trimming up ears and noses. "I been needing some cuticle scissors."

"Listen, Crunch, we need a plan of action," O'Leary said. "It won't do us any good to just go blundering out of here and wind up back in chains. The palace is swarming with guards, Rodolpho's regular staff plus Goruble's strongarm squad. We need a diversion—something to distract attention while I sneak in and whisk Swinehild and Lady Andragorre out from under his nose."

"Hey!" a reedy voice yelled from a side passage. "I demand a lawyer! I want to see the American consul! I have a right to make a phone call!"

"That sounds like Lorenzo . . ."

Lafayette trotted along to the cell from which the shouts had come. A nattily Vandycked and moustached fellow with an Edgar Allan Poe haircut and a high, stiff collar by Hoover out of Napoleon was gripping the bars with well-manicured hands.

"You, there . . ." His voice trailed off. "Say don't I know you?"

"Lorenzo?" Lafayette eyed the other. "Got

caught after all, eh? The last I saw of you, you were leaving me in the lurch with a free run ahead, but of course you blew it. And where'd you get the beaver and the fancy outfit?"

"Don't babble," the prisoner snapped in the same annoying fashion Lafayette had listened to in the dark cell under the Glass Tree. "My name's Lafcadio, not that it's any of your business. Say, who are you, anyway? I'd swear we've met somewhere . . ."

"This is no time to play games," Lafayette snapped. "Crunch and I broke out. I'm going to make a try for the Lady Andragorre, but—"

"You mean Cynthia, I suppose. Are you in on this fantastic plot too? Well, you won't get away with it! And stay away from my fiancée—"

"I thought her name was Beverly. But let's skip that. If I get you out, will you help create a diversion to cover my movements?"

"Just get me out," the bearded inmate yelped. "We can talk about terms later."

"Crunch!" Lafayette called. "See to this door, will you?" He went on along the passage. Most of the prisoners slumped on their straw pallets, but a few watched him with alert eyes.

"Listen, men," he called. "We're breaking out! If I free you, will your promise to run amok in the corridors, attack the guards, smash things, yell, and generally commit a nuisance?"

"Hey—you're on, mister!"

"That's for me!"

"Count me in!"

"Swell." Lafayette hurried back to instruct Crunch. Moments later the giant was busily dismantling the cellblock. Bushy-bearded villains of all degrees of dishevelment crowded into the torture chamber. Lafayette caught a glimpse of Lorenzo, now minus his disguise. He pushed through to him.

"Listen, why don't you and I work together . . ." He paused, staring at his former roommate, who was staring back with a puzzled expression on his features—features which O'Leary was seeing clearly in an adequate light for the first time.

"Hey," Crunch boomed. "I thought you went thataway, palsy . . ." He broke off. "Uh . . ." He hesitated, looking from Lafayette to the other man. "Say, maybe I'm losing my bite—but which one o' youse birds is my pal which we just sprung out together?"

"I'm Lafayette," O'Leary spoke up. "This is Lorenzo—"

"Nonsense, my name is Lothario—and I never saw this pithecanthropus before in my life." He looked Crunch up and down.

"Why'n'cha say youse had a twin brother?" Crunch inquired.

"Twin brother?" both men said as one.

"Yeah. And listen, little chum: what was you doing dressed up in buckskins and knee boots? What are youse, a quick-change artist?"

Lafayette was staring at Lorenzo's—or Lothario's—clothing: a skin-tight doublet and hose, topped by a brocaded tailcoat and a ruffled shirt, all much the worse for wear.

"He doesn't look like me," he said indignantly. "Oh, there might be some superficial resemblance—but I don't have that feckless look, that irresponsible expression—"

"Me look like you?" the other was exclaiming.

"You haven't known me long enough to be handing out insults. Now, where's the nearest imperial transfer booth? You can depend on it, I'm turning in a report to my PR rep that will clean out this whole nest of hebephrenics before you can say 'noblesse oblige!' "

"You there!" A shout cut through the hubbub. "Lafayette!" He turned. A man identical but for clothing to the one with whom he was conversing was pushing through the press toward him, waving his arm. Lafayette whirled. The man who had called himself Lothario was gone in the milling crowd.

"How did you get here?" Lorenzo was demanding as he came up. "I'm glad to see you got clear. Say, I never got a chance to thank you for saving me from Krupkin's men. Beverly told me what happened, poor kid. She was so confused by everything that she didn't even remember my name—"

"What is your name?" Lafayette cut in with a rising sense of imminent paranoia.

"Huh? Why, it's Lorenzo, of course!"

Lafayette stared at the face before him, noting the set of the blue eyes, the untamed lock of brownish-blond hair over the forehead, the well-shaped mouth marred by a certain petulance. . . .

"What's . . ." He stopped to swallow. "What's your last name?"

"O'Leary, why?" Lorenzo said.

"Lorenzo O'Leary," Lafayette mumbled. "I should have known. If Adoranne and Daphne and Yockabump and Nicodaeus all had doubles here—why not me?"

Twelve

"Hey, chums!" Crunch's subcellar voice shattered the paralysis that gripped the two O'Learys. "It's time to blow, if we don't want to miss all the fun." Lafayette looked around, saw that the room was rapidly emptying as the shouting mob of released prisoners streamed away along the passage, brandishing rude implements pressed into service from the array racked around the walls.

"Look, Lorenzo—we can sort out who's who later," he said over the fading clamor. "Right now the important thing is to save poor Swinehild and the Lady Andragorre from Goruble—Krupkin, to you. He's hatched a mad plot to take over Artesia, and the lousy part of it is, it looks as though he may be able to do it. No wonder he didn't care much whether I helped him or not: He can ring you in for me and force Swinehild to cooperate, and—but never mind that. I'm going to try to reach Rodolpho's apartment and tell him what's going on. Maybe it's still not too late to nip the whole thing in the bud. Why don't you come with me? Maybe between the two of us, one will get through. I'll brief you on the way. How about it?"

"Well—since you seem to have some notion of

what's going on in this cackle factory, I may as well—but keep your meat hooks off Beverly!"

"I thought her name was Cynthia," Lafayette muttered as they selected stout clubs from a handy club stand and set off behind Crunch in the wake of the mob. Ahead, startled yells and a rising roar of enthusiasm indicated first contact with the palace guard.

"Down here," Lafayette called, indicating a side passage. "We'll go around, try for the back stairs."

"Look here, where do you fit into all this?" Lorenzo panted as they raced along the winding corridor.

"I don't," Lafayette assured his double. "I was back in Artesia, minding my own business, when suddenly here I was in Melange. The next thing I knew, I was up to my neck in accusations—" He veered aside into a stairway leading up. "I guess that was your doing; they mistook me for you, apparently. You must have been pretty busy, judging from the way the cops jumped me."

"It looked like a fairly straightforward proposition," Lorenzo puffed, keeping pace as they bounded up the steps, Crunch slogging along in the rear. "Krupkin . . . offered me a free trip home . . . plus other inducements such as staying alive . . . if I'd carry out a mission for him. I was supposed to sneak myself into . . . this Lady Andragorre's chamber . . . and set up a tryst. Well . . . I climbed a few walls . . . and paid a few bribes . . . I got in, all right. But then . . . I saw it was Beverly. We didn't have time to talk much . . . but I did slip her a note . . . proposing a rendezvous at the cottage—as Krupkin had

planned. But from there on I intended to intro-
duce . . . some changes . . . in the script. . . ."

"He suckered you," Lafayette panted. "I don't
know how he got you here . . . but I doubt if he
had any intention . . . of sending you back to
your United Colonies. . . ."

They emerged from the stairhead into a wide
corridor, from both ends of which sounds of mob
violence rose.

"Let's see—I think it's that way," Lafayette
pointed. As they sprang forward, there was a bel-
low from behind them. Crunch was rubbing his
head and looking back down the stairway.

"Why, the lousy bums—" he roared, and dived
back down the steps.

"Crunch!" Lafayette yelled, but the giant was
gone. A moment later, a tremendous crash
sounded from the stairwell, followed by sounds of
hand-to-hand combat.

"Let's get out of here," Lorenzo proposed, and
dashed for the grand staircase ahead. Lafayette
followed. A guard in crimson popped into view
above, brought up a blunderbuss to firing position—

"Don't shoot that thing, you idiot!" Lorenzo
yelled. "You'll louse up the wallpaper!" While
the confused sentry was still blinking, the two
fugitives struck him amidships; as he went down,
the piece discharged a load of birdshot into the
floral-patterned ceiling.

"I told you not to spoil the wallpaper," Lorenzo
said as he bounced the man's head on the floor
and bounded on. They ascended another two
flights, pelted along a carpeted passage happily
deserted of guards, to the door Lafayette remem-

bered from his last visit. The sounds of battle were
faint here. They skidded to a halt, drew a few
gulps of air.

"Now, let me do the talking, Lorenzo,"
Lafayette panted. "Rodolpho and I are old drink-
ing buddies—"

A door twenty feet along the hall flew open;
flanked by four burly crimson-uniformed men,
the short, imperious figure of Krupkin/Goruble
strutted forth, turned to speak back over his
shoulder: "That's an order, not a suggestion,
Rudy! Present yourself and your chief ministers
in the Grand Ballroom in half an hour, prepared to
rubber-stamp my mobilization, curfew, rationing,
and martial-law proclamations, or find yourself
dangling from your own castle walls!" The former
usurper of Artesia twitched his ermine-edged
robes into line and strode off along the passage,
conveyed by his bodyguard.

"So much for Rodolpho's help," Lorenzo muttered. "Any other ideas?"

Lafayette frowned, nibbled his lip. "You know
where this ballroom is?"

"Two flights up, on the south side."

"It would be; that's where the riot's centered, to
judge from the sounds of shattering glass."

"So what?" Lorenzo inquired. "It sounds like a
swell place to stay clear of. We can dodge around
to Beverly's apartment and grab her off while the
big shots are playing politics."

"I have reason to believe Daph—I mean Lady
Andragorre will be in the ballroom, along with
Swinehild. It's all part of Goruble's big plan. We
have to stop him now, before things go any farther."

"How? There's just the two of us. What can we do against a whole palace full of armed men?"

"I don't know—but we have to try! Come on! If we can't get through one way, we'll find another—and time's a-wasting!"

Twenty-five of the allotted thirty minutes had passed. Lafayette and Lorenzo crouched on the palace roof, thirty feet above the high windows of the ballroom two floors below. Already the murmur of nervous conversation rose to them from the chamber where great events were about to occur.

"All right," Lafayette said. "Who goes first, you or me?"

"We'll both be killed," Lorenzo said, peering over the parapet. "The cornice overhangs about three feet. It's impossible—"

"All right, I'll go first. If I . . ." Lafayette paused to swallow. "If I fall, take up where I left off. Remember, Lady Andragorre—I mean Beverly's counting on you." He mounted the low wall rimming the roof, and carefully avoiding looking down, prepared to lower himself over the edge.

"Hold it!" Lorenzo said. "That metal edging looks sharp. It might cut the rope. We'll have to pad it . . ."

"Here, use my coat." Lafayette stripped off the gaudy garment given to him by the employees of the Ajax works, folded it, tucked it under the rope they had purloined from a utility room under the eaves.

"And we really need some stout leather gauntlets," Lorenzo pointed out. "And shin guards. And spiked shoes would help."

"Sure—and it would be nice if we had large insurance policies," Lafayette cut him off. "Since we don't, we'd better get moving before our resolve stiffens up on us." He gripped the rope, gritted his teeth, and slid down into windy darkness.

The wind clawed at his coatless back. His feet pawed for nonexistent purchase on the wall three feet away. The fibers of the heavy rope rasped at his palms like barbed wire. The lighted window below slid closer. His foot touched the wall with a noise which seemed loud enough to rouse the county. Ignoring the ache in his arms, the quivering in his stomach, the sense of bottomless depths yawning below, Lafayette inched down the last few feet, came to rest dangling against the four-foot section of blank wall between two windows. From inside came a restless susurrus of voices, the shuffle of feet.

". . . can't imagine what it's about," a male tenor was exclaiming. "Unless it's my investiture as Squire of Honor to the Ducal Manicure coming through at last . . ."

"Gracious knows it's about time my appointment as Second Honorary Tonsorial Artist in Attendance on the Ducal Moustache was confirmed," a fruity baritone averred. "But what a curious hour for the cermony . . ."

"Since his Grace has no moustache, you may be waiting quite a while, Fauntley," an acid voice suggested. "But—hark—they're coming . . ."

"Sst! Are you all right?" Lorenzo's call hissed from above. Lafayette craned upward, could see nothing but the dark bulk of the overhanging cornice.

From inside sounded a flourish of trumpets. There was a spatter of polite handclapping, followed by a sonorous announcement in an incomprehensible nasal. Then Duke Rodolpho's reedy voice spoke up faintly: ". . . gathered here . . . this auspicious occasion . . . pleasure and honor to present . . . a few words . . . careful attention. . . ."

More polite applause, then a sudden hush.

"I'll not mince words," Goruble's voice rang out. "A state of dire emergency exists. Prompt measures are called for . . ." As the voice droned on, the rope to which O'Leary clung began to shake. Seconds later, Lorenzo appeared, descending rapidly.

"Slow down!" Lafayette hissed, as a pair of sharp-cornered boots slammed against his shoulders, dug in with crushing weight on his clavicles.

"Hssst, Lafayette! Where are you?"

"You're standing on me, you idiot!" Lafayette managed between teeth clenched in agony. "Get off!"

"Get off?" Lorenzo hissed back. "Onto what?"

"I don't care what! Just do it—before I lose my grip and we both go down!"

There were huffings and puffings from above. One foot lifted from O'Leary's pained flesh, then the other.

"All right—I'm clinging like a human fly to a crack you couldn't hide a dime in," Lorenzo whispered shakily. "Now what?"

"Shut up and listen!"

". . . for this reason, I have decided to honor the lady in question by making her my bride,"

Goruble was announcing in unctuous tones. "You
have been chosen to witness this felicitous event
as an indication of my high esteem for your loyalty, to say nothing of your keen judgment, which
tells you when to join in the spirit of the occasion." He paused ominously. "Now, is there anyone present who knows of any reason why I
should not be instantly joined in holy matrimony
to the Lady Andragorre?"

"Why, the dirty, double-crossing rat!"
Lafayette burst out.

"Why, you dirty, double-crossing rat!" an
angry shout sounded from within—in the unmis-
takable tones of Duke Rodolpho. "This wasn't
part of our agreement, you slimy little upstart!"

"Seize the traitor!" Goruble bellowed.

"What's happening?" Lorenzo whispered as
bedlam broke out within.

"Krupkin plans to marry Lady Andragorre, the
swindler! Rodolpho is objecting, and Krupkin's
objecting to his objecting!"

The babble from within had risen to a clamor
reminiscent of a traffic jam. Goruble's shouted
orders mingled with screams, curses, Rodolpho's
bellows of outrage. There was a scrape and a
crunch, and Lorenzo was jostling Lafayette on his
fragile perch.

"Out of the way," he yelled. "Just wait until I
get my hands on that kidnapping, confidence-
betraying, bride-stealing son of a rachitic fry
cook!"

"Hey," Lafayette yelled as his fellow eaves-
dropper thrust against him, nearly dislodging
him from his grip. "Hold on!"

"I'll hold on—onto his neck, the lousy little

claim-jumper!" Lorenzo's swinging boot contacted glass; it burst in with an explosive crash. An instant later the enraged Lorenzo had disappeared through the swirling drapes.

"The poor idot!" Lafayette groaned. "He'll be torn to bits—and without helping Daphne—I mean Beverly—I mean Cynthia—or Lady Andragorre at all!" He craned, caught a glimpse of the surging crowd, the red-uniformed men moving among the gowns and cravats, of Lorenzo, charging through—

At the last moment, Goruble turned—in time to receive a jolting roundhouse punch in the right eye. As the assaulted prince staggered back, large uniforms loomed, closed in on Lorenzo.

"That did it," Lafayette muttered. "But at least he landed one good one . . ." He leaned for another look.

"So," Goruble was roaring, dabbing at his injured eye with a large lace-edged hanky, "it's you, is it, Lorenzo? I have plans for you, lad! Gorog's been fed once this evening, but he'll savor another snack, no doubt! And before you die, you'll have the pleasure of witnessing my union with the lady whom you've had the audacity to molest with your unwanted attentions!"

"M-M-Milady Andragorre," the shaken voice of a palace footman announced in the sudden hush. The crowd parted. A dark-haired, dark-eyed vision of loveliness appeared, clad in bridal white, accompanied by a pair of angular females in bridesmaid's costume which failed to conceal their police-matronly physiques.

"On with the ceremony," Goruble shouted, all pretense of courtliness gone now. "Tonight, my nuptials; tomorrow, the conquest of the known universe!"

Lafayette clung to the wall, shivering violently as the icy wind whipped at his shirt. His hands were as numb as grappling hooks, though far less secure. His toes felt like frozen shrimp. Any moment now, his clutch would fail, and down he would go, into the depths below. He pressed his chin against the cold stone, listening to the droning voice of the ecclesiastic beyond the window, intoning the marriage ceremony.

"Why did it have to end like this?" he muttered. "Why did I have to get mixed up in it in the first place? Why didn't Pratwick help me instead of torturing me with that idiotic jingle—that meaningless rhyme that doesn't rhyme? ". . . the favorite of millions from the Bronx to Miami The key to the riddle is . . . what? What rhymes with 'Miami'? 'Mammy'? 'Bon Ami'? 'Clammy'? The favorite of millions from the Bronx to Miami—the key to the riddle is . . . is . . ."

There was a sudden outburst inside: "Beverly—tell him no! Even if he does promise to slit my throat if you don't go through with it!" Lorenzo's shout was cut off by a meaty smack followed by a thud.

"He's merely stunned, my dear," Goruble said unctuously. "Carry on, you!"

"D-do you . . . Lady Andragorre . . . take this . . . this Prince . . ."

"No," Lafayette moaned. "This is too terrible. It couldn't be happening! Total, utter failure—and I've always been such a lucky fellow—like finding the door in the cliff when I needed it, and the

Mad Monk costume, and . . . and . . ." He froze, groping for a ghostly idea floating just beyond his grasp.

"Think," he commanded himself. "Luck, I've been calling it. But that's fantastic. You don't have that kind of luck. That's the kind of thing that happens when you manipulate the probability fabric. So—the conclusion is that you were manipulating the cosmic energies. It worked—those times. But other times it didn't. But what was the difference? What did those occasions have in common that was lacking when I tried and failed?"

"Smelling salts," Goruble was bellowing from inside. "The poor creature's fainted, no doubt from the sheer thrill of her good fortune . . ."

"Nothing," Lafayette groaned. "I can't think of a thing. All I can think of is poor Daphne, and Swinehild, a sweet kid even if she did smell like garlic. . . .

Garlic. . . .

"Garlic's always been associated with thaumaturgy and spells," Lafayette babbled, grasping at straws. "And spells are just amateur efforts to manipulate the cosmic energies! Could it be garlic? Or maybe Swinehild herself—but 'Swinehild' doesn't rhyme with 'Miami.' Neither does 'garlic.' Anyway, she only smelled like garlic because she was always making sandwiches out of that kosher salami—

"Kosher salami!" Lafayette shouted. "That's it! The favorite of millions from the Bronx to Miami—the key to the riddle is kosher salami!" He gulped, almost lost his grip, grabbed and held on.

"The salami was under me when I conjured up the knife—and we were eating it when I managed the costumes—and it was in my pocket on the cliff. So all I have to do is—"

O'Leary felt a cold hand clutch his heart.

"My pocket. It was in the pocket of my coat— and I left it up above, padding the rope!

"All right," he answered. "So that means you have a climb ahead, that's all.

"Climb up there? My hands are like ice, and I'm weak as a kitten, and freezing, and anyway—it will take too long—

"Get moving.

"I . . . I'll try." With vast effort, O'Leary unclamped a hand, groped for a grip higher up on the rope. He was dangling free of the wall now. His arms were like bread dough, he realized, his weight like a lead effigy.

"It's no use . . .

"Try!"

Somehow he pulled up another foot. Somehow he managed another six inches. He clung, resting, inches upward. The wind banged him against the wall. He looked up; something dark lay on the parapet, flapping in the wind.

"It's too far," he gasped. "And anyway—" As he watched with horrified fascination, the coat, having gradually worked free of the rope under which it had been pinned, flopped over, the brocaded tails dangling down the outer face of the parapet. The wind plucked at the garment, nudged it closer to the edge. It hung for a moment; a new gust stirred it—

It was falling, the empty sleeves waving a hectic

farewell, dropping toward him. Wind-tossed, it whirled out away from the building.

With a wild lunge, Lafayette threw himself into space. His outstretched fingertips brushed the coat, snatched, caught the heavy cloth. As wild wind screamed past him, O'Leary groped for the pocket; his fingers closed over the greasy lump of salami Swinehild had placed there—

"A miracle! Any miracle! But make it fast!"

A terrific blow smashed at O'Leary; out of the darkness he went spinning end over end into fire-shot darkness filled with shatterings and smashing and screams. Then blackness closed in like a filled grave.

"It was a miracle," a voice that Lafayette remembered from another lifetime, ages before, was saying. "As I reconstruct events, he fell from the roof, struck the flagpole, and was catapulted back up and through the window, to land squarely atop his Highness, who was rushing to discover the source of the curious sounds outside."

"Give him air," another voice snapped.

Lafayette found his eyes open, looking up at the frowning visage of Lorenzo, somewhat bruised but as truculent as ever.

"You could at least have let me in on your plan," the other O'Leary said. "I was getting worried there at the last, just before you arrived."

"You . . . you were marvelous, sir," a sweet voice murmured. With an effort like pushing boulders, Lafayette shifted his eyes, was looking into the smiling face of Daphne—or Lady Andragorre, he corrected himself with a pang of homesickness.

"You . . . really don't know me, do you?" O'Leary managed to chirp weakly.

"You're wondrous like one I know well, yclept Lancelot," the lady said softly. "I ween 'twas you I saw from my coach as I rode forth to my tryst in the forest. But—no, fair sir. We are strangers . . . and I am all the more in your debt."

"As am I," another voice spoke up. A man stood beside Lady Andragorre, his arm familiarly around her girlish waist. He wore a short, trimmed beard and a curling moustache under a floppy hat. "Methought I'd languish till dooms-day in his Grace's dungeons—until you arrived to spring me." He studied Lafayette's face, frown-ing. "Though I cannot for my life see this fancied resemblance of which my bride prates."

"Face it, Lafayette," Lorenzo spoke up. "This character's in on the ground floor. He belongs here in Melange, it seems. He used to be duke, before Krupkin came along and stuck Rodolpho up in his place. Now he's in charge again, and Krupkin's in the dungeon. And the lady isn't Bev-erly after all. She finally convinced me." He sighed. "So—I guess we lose out."

"Swinehild," Lafayette muttered, and managed to sit up. "Is she all right?"

"I'm here—and in the pink, thanks to you, Lafe," the former barmaid cried, elbowing a nervous-looking medico aside. "Gee, sugar, you look terrible." She smiled down at him, radiant in her court costume.

"I just want to talk to her!" a shrill male voice was yelling in the background. A ruffled figure in tight silks thrust through the circle, shot Lafayette a hot look, confronted Lady Andragorre.

"What's this all about, Eronne? Who's this bewhiskered Don Juan who's fingering your hipbone? And where did you get that get-up? What is this place? What's going on—"

"Hold it, chum," Lorenzo said, taking the stranger's elbow. "This is going to take a little explaining, but it seems we're all in the same boat—"

"Get lost, junior; who asked you to meddle?" The newcomer jerked his sleeve free. "Well, what about it, Eronne?" he addressed Lady Andragorre. "You act as if you'd never seen me before! It's me, Lothario O'Leary, your intended, remember?"

"The lady's name is Andragorre," the moustached Duke Lancelot spoke up harshly. "And she happens to be my intended, not yours!"

"Oh, yeah?"

"Absolutely! Wouldst dispute me?"

As peacemakers moved in to soothe the ruffled disputants, Lafayette rose unsteadily, and, supported by Swinehild, tottered away.

"I have to get out of here," he said. "Look, Swinehild—I've had a stroke of luck at last. I've recovered my ability to manipulate the cosmic energies—so I'm going home, where I belong. And I wonder—well, I have Daphne waiting for me, so I don't want you to misunderstand my motives—but wouldn't you like to come with me? I can pass you off as a long-lost cousin of Adoranne's, and with a little tutoring in how to walk and talk, you can soon fit right in—"

"Gee, Lafe—you really gotta go?"

"Certainly! But as I said, you may come too. So if you're ready—"

"Uh, say, excuse me, ma'am," a deep voice aid hesitantly. "Begging your ladyship's pardon, but I was looking for—I mean, I hear tell my, er, wife—what I mean to say is, I plan to get around to marrying her as soon as . . ."

"Hulk!" Swinehild cried. "You come looking for me! You must care!"

"Swinehild?" Hulk quavered incredulously. "H-holy jumping Georgie Jessel—you're—you're plumb beautiful!"

"Hmmmphh," Lafayette said as the pair moved off, grabbing at each other. He managed to work his way across the room unnoticed, slipped out into a small cloakroom off the grand ballroom.

"Home," he said, patting his pockets. "Home sweet home . . ." He frowned, patted his pockets again, in turn. "Damn! I've lost the salami . . . must have dropped it somewhre between the flagstaff and Goruble's head." He reemerged, encountered Lorenzo.

"There you are!" his double exclaimed. "Look here, Lafayette—we have to talk! Maybe between the two of us we can summon up enough cosmic power to get back where we belong! I'm going crackers watching Duke Lancelot squeeze Andragorre—"

"Just help me find my salami," Lafayette countered. "Then I'll see what I can do."

"Food, at a time like this?" But he followed as Lafayette led the way down into the courtyard directly below the scene of his miraculous coup of an hour before.

"It should be lying around here some-place . . ."

"For heaven's sake, why not go to the kitchen?"

"Look, Lorenzo, I know it sounds silly, but this salami is vital to my psychic-energy-harnessing. Don't ask me why—ask a bureaucrat named Pratwick."

Ten minutes' diligent search of the enclosed space yielded no salami.

"Listen, was I holding it in my hand when I came through the window?" he inquired urgently of Lorenzo.

"How would I know, I had two bruisers sitting on my chest at the time. I didn't know what was happening until that Lancelot character came charging in and demanded the return of his ducal estates."

"We'll have to go back up and ask." Back in the ballroom, now only sparsely crowded as the former adherents of the now-imprisoned Rodolpho maneuvered for position in the entourage of their new master, Lafayette went about plucking at sleeves, repeating his question. He netted nothing but blank stares and a few polite laughs.

"A blank," he said as Lorenzo, equally luckless, rejoined him. "To think I had it that close—and let it get away."

"What's up, Lafe," Swinehild spoke behind him. "Lost something?"

"Swinehild—the kosher salami from our lunch—have you seen it?"

"Nope. But wait a minute, I'll see if Hulk's got some. He loves the stuff."

Hulk sauntered over, wiping his mouth. "Somebody call me?" he inquired, and belched. "Par' me," he said. "Kosher salami gives me gas."

Lafayette sniffed. "You didn't—you didn't *eat* it?"

"Was that yours, Mister O'Leary? Sorry about that. Can't get any more just like it, but we got plenty liverwurst back at Ye Beggar's Bole."

"That does it," Lafayette moaned. "I'm sunk. I'm stuck here forever." He slumped in a chair, put his face in his hands. "Daphne," he muttered. "Will I ever see you again?" He groaned, remembering her as he had seen her last, her voice, the way she moved, the touch of her hand. . . .

The room had grown curiously still. Lafayette opened his eyes. A few dropped hankies and smeared cigar butts on the polished floor were all that remained to indicate that a few moments before a noisy crowd had thronged the room. Faintly, voices floated from the passage outside. Lafayette sprang up, ran to the high, ornately carved, silver-handled door, pushed through into the red-carpeted hall. A figure—he thought it was Lothario, or possibly Lorenzo—was just disappearing around the shadowy corner. He called but no one answered. He hurried along the empty passage, looked into rooms.

"Swinehild!" he called. "Lorenzo! Anybody!"

Only echoes answered him.

"It's happened again," he whispered. "Everyone's disappeared, and left me marooned. Why? How?"

A sound of padding feet approaching along a side passage. A small, rotund figure in green-leather pants and a plaid sportcoat appeared at the head of a band of Ajax men.

"Sprawnroyal!" O'Leary greeted the customer-service man. "Thank Grunk someone's left alive here!"

"Hello, Slim. Boy, you get around. Me and the boys are here to see Krupkin—"

"He's in the dungeon—"

"Say, we're operating a half-phase out of sync with Melange; we usually duck over here for jobs like this to avoid the crowd, you know. But how'd you get here? When your Mark XIII come back empty, we thought you'd bought the farm! And—"

"It's a long story—but listen. I just had a thought of blinding brilliance! Krupkin gave you plans for a Traveler. Will you build it—for me—so I can go back to Artesia, and—"

"Not a chance, friend." Sprawnroyal held up both hands in negation. "If we pulled a trick like that, Central would land on us like a ton of twenty-two-karat uranium bricks!"

"Central! That's it! Put me in touch with Central, so I can explain what happened, and—"

"Nix again, Slim. Pinchcraft just got through going round and round with some paper-pusher named Fernwick or something about an allegation Ajax had let slip some cosmic-total-secret info to Krupkin. We barely managed to square matters; we won't reopen that can of worms for a while, believe me!"

"But—where is everybody?"

"We told Central about some of the monkey business going on here. Seems like Krupkin used stuff we sold him to make up a gadget to meddle with the probability fabric. He used it to yank a fellow named Lorenzo here. Wanted to use him as bait to get his hands on Lady A, so he could trade her back for Rodolpho's help. But when he did, he started a chain reaction; he got Lorenzo, and a couple dozen other troublemakers from alternate realities. What a hassle! But Central pulled a few strings and whisked a lot of displaced characters back to where they belonged. I don't know how it is they left you stranded here in half-phase. There's no life here at all, you know."

Lafayette leaned against the wall and closed his eyes. "I'm doomed," he muttered. "They're all against me. But maybe—maybe if I go back to Ajax with you, and explain matters directly to Pinch-craft and the others, they'll think of something."

Suddenly the silence was suspicious. O'Leary snapped his eyes open. Sprawnroyal was gone. The corridor was empty. There was not even an impress of feet in the deep-pile blue carpet to show where he had stood.

"Blue carpet?" he muttered dazedly. "But I thought it was red. The only place I've seen a blue carpet like this was in Lod's palace . . ."

He whirled and ran along the corridor, leaped down stairs, sprinted across a wide lobby, dashed out onto an expanse of sand-drifted lawn, turned to look back. Broken lavender neon letters spelled out LAS VEGAS HILTON.

"It's it," he gobbled. "The building Goruble supplied to Lod. And that means—I'm back in Artesia . . . doesn't it?" He looked out across the dark expanse of desert. "Or am I still in some kind of never-never land?"

"There's just one way to find out," he told himself. "There's twenty miles of loose sand between here and the capital. Start walking."

Dawn was bleaching the sky ahead as Lafayette

tottered the last few yards to the door of the One-Eyed Man tavern on the west post road.

"Red Bull," he whispered hoarsely, thumping feebly at the heavy panel. "Let me in . . ."

There was no response from behind the shuttered windows. An icy chill stirred in Lafayette's midsection.

"It's deserted," he muttered. "A ghost city, an empty continuum. They shifted me out of Melange, because I was unbalancing the probability equation, but instead of sending me home they marooned me . . ."

He hobbled on through the empty streets. Ahead was the high wall surrounding the palace grounds. He clung for a moment to the small service gate, then, with fear in his heart, thrust it open.

Morning mist hung among brooding trees. Dew glistened on silent grass. Far away, an early bird called. Beyond the manicured flower beds, the rose-marble palace loomed, soundless. No curtain fluttered from an open window. No cheery voices cried greetings. No footstep sounded on the flagged walks.

"Gone," O'Leary whispered. "All gone . . ."

He walked like a man in a dream across the wet grass, past the fountain, where a tiny trickle of water tinkled. His favorite bench was just ahead. He would sit there awhile, and then . . .

And then . . . he didn't know.

There was the flowering arbutus; the bench was just beyond. He rounded it—

She was sitting on the bench, a silvery shawl about her slim shoulders, holding a rosebud in her fingers. She turned, looked up at him. The prettiest face in the known universe opened into a smile like a flower bursting into blossom.

"Lafayette! You've come back!"

"Daphne . . . I . . . I . . . you . . ."

Then she was in his arms.